THE HOUMAN RACE:

BIRTH

Warren Cohen, Jr.

Published by CreateSpace Independent Publishing Platform; 2nd edition (August 22, 2013)

- ISBN-10: 1481829416
- ISBN-13: 978-1481829410

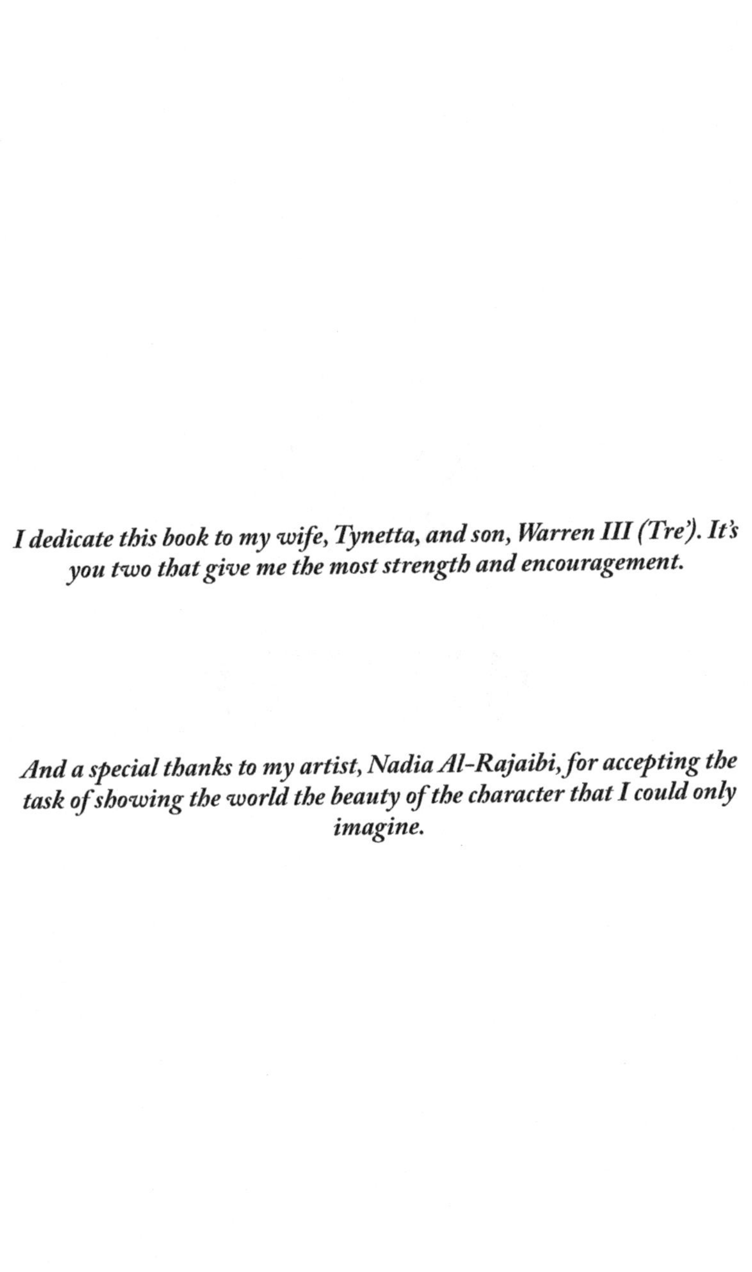

I dedicate this book to my wife, Tynetta, and son, Warren III (Tre'). It's you two that give me the most strength and encouragement.

And a special thanks to my artist, Nadia Al-Rajaibi, for accepting the task of showing the world the beauty of the character that I could only imagine.

THE HOUMAN RACE:

BIRTH

THE LAND OF CHOI

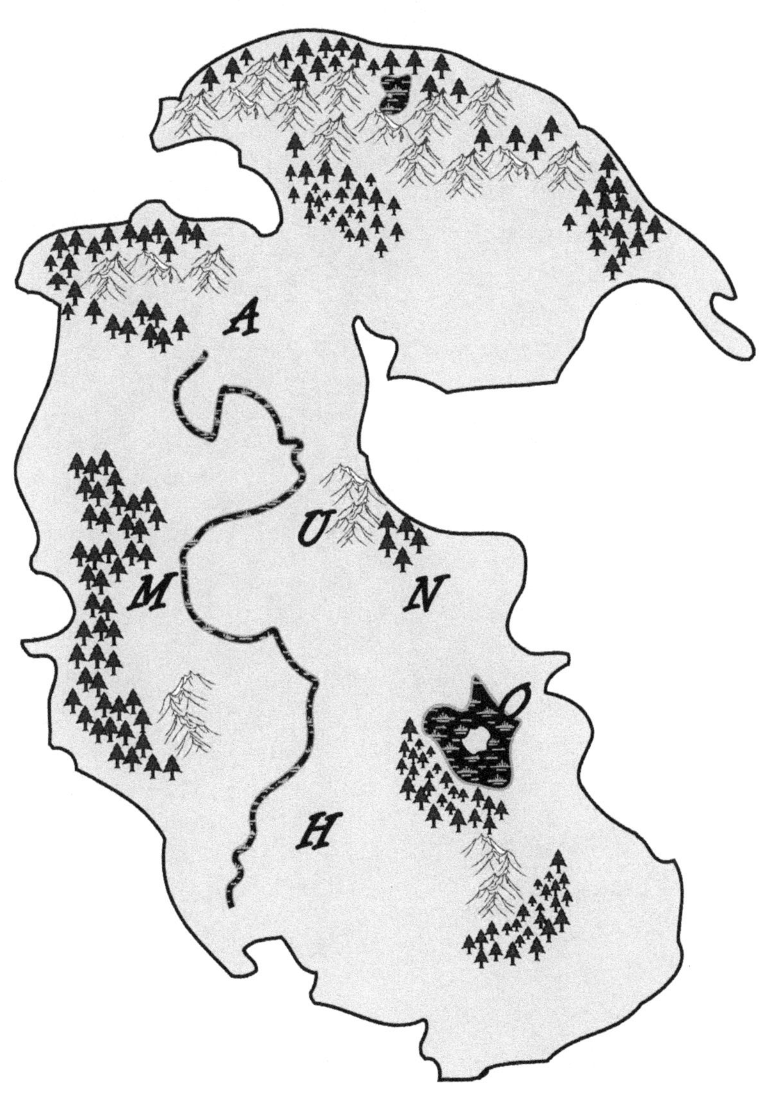

PROLOGUE

It was the year 2015, and the world had come to chaos. Nations, once allies, were turning on each other. Each country decided to rely on its own resources, virtually depleting international importing. Fueled by anger, poverty, and power, each nation went looking for anything to tip the balance in their favor. History is still unsure which country released their bomb first, or even why, but before it could land, ten others were launched in retaliation. It obliterated over eight-five percent of the planet. It became known as Day TX: Total Extinction.

As it always does without major human interference, the world healed. It grew, and prospered. Trees and animals repopulated and thrived. Forests grew and cleaned the air. The acidic water, after years of raining torment eventually cleaned itself out. Humans, the few that survived, even began to grow and learn again. However this growth was slow. Without technology humans were regressed as species. They were so low in numbers that many became nomadic to search for food and other cities. Even the term city had become foreign and considered ancient knowledge. It was as if Day TX was also the restart of the human race, just somewhat smarter than the first time. It caused people to learn something time made them forget, how to be human again.

Hundreds of years passed. And like history shows

as humans migrated and grew in size so did war and violence. Clans gathered and turned into villages, and each village tried to outdo the others. Eventually neighboring villages would also band together and form cloisters. In the year 942TX, a young teenager named Hikothe was studying his father's books. He loved reading and learning all he could. It was one particular day that he found an old book about dragons. It told of their history and demise. It gave examples of how to care for them, train them, feed them, and properly treat them. Most importantly, it told of how to find and hatch them. It was the greatest book he ever read. Then alongside it was another book on Human history. Hikothe, fourteen years old, read both books. He then read them multiple times over. He committed to learning their contents entirely.

Hikothe searched for years trying to put together the exact locations the book foretold, and then one day he finally found one of the hidden eggs. It was as large as a dog and colored blue with dark gold streaks stretching outward from the opposite ends. It had taken two years for him to find the right waterfall and cave he learned from the book. Then, using the book as a reference he loosened the beautiful egg to be hatched. It was like seeing the sun after years of rain. Hikothe, back against the cave wall, told the dragon his name as he saw blue scaled claws breaking out of the shell. Startled and agitated from the new experience he hid and peered from behind a large wet rock. The drake broke through his once eternal resting place. He looked around and smelled the air. The large blue lizard turned in the teen's direction and began walking over. Hikothe was tense, fearful of losing his life, until the freshly hatched drake said "Thank you Hikothe, my name is Hikarge, and we have much to discuss." Hikothe gave him the two large rabbits he captured that same morning. Realizing the rabbits would not be enough, he gave Hikarge the remaining food he prepared for his travel. They then spent the entire night talking. It was the day everything changed in TX. It was the day dragons re-entered the world.

BEFORE TIME KNEW HOUMANS

One day, a young dragon tender was looking through his father's old books and came across an old dusty one called ***The Houman Race***. He was perplexed at the spelling of human and began to read it. The pages were worn and tattered, so most of it he could not read. He decided to take it to his grandfather, the eldest dragon rider of his village. His Grandfather, Hikothe, was not only the elder of his village, but was also the Dama of all nine villages, the cloister of Aimone.

Each village had an elder that lorded over it. In many cases, more so than not, a group of villages, ranging from three to twenty-five, would band together and form a cloister to create a stronger kingdom. In this cloister, there would be a sole ruler, called a Dama. Each village elder would inherit the position on the king's council, the Dama Regent. The Dama would most times be awarded to the strongest man in the cloister of villages at its forming, and then passed down by lineage. Hikothe, the eldest and strongest dragon rider of Aimone used his time to bring not only peace and prosperity to his cloister, but also a wealth of knowledge.

"Hikune, my grandson, what goodies have you come for today?" asked Hikothe of his youngest grandson. "I see you have been going through my library again. And by the book in your hand and the smile on your face, I am to understand it is something wonderful."

"I found a weird book grandfather!" Hikune yelled excitedly as he ran towards his destination. "I can't read it, but was hoping you would be able to explain it to me with your extensive knowledge. You know everything in the library." Upon reaching his grandfather, he paused to catch his breath. Then he quickly handed the old book over to his boisterous grandfather.

Hikothe's eyes looked down on the book and immediately a shallow darkness entered his eyes. Yet with that solemn look came a smile of joy as well as sorrow. "And what is it you would like to know of this book Hikune?" inquired Hikothe. "It is quite old and I'm not entirely sure you would want to know of its contents, or if I can accurately tell it to you in my old age"

Hikune looked with sadness at his solemn grandfather. "Please tell me, that is, if you can grandfather. It looks weird with that spelling of "human" on in. It must be a mistake, but a book that large couldn't have been printed with such a mistake in the title. There are so many questions I have. I really want to know. It may help me become a better dragon tender, and even a better rider someday."

With seeing the hopefulness and determination to know the truth in his grandson, Hikothe let out a small chuckle. "Okay Hikune, second son of my only son, I will tell you what is in this book. Some say it is a book as old as the human race, though I doubt that it is. However, it is not just a story book, but a history book. The book is one about the true human race and how we came to be as we are now. Yet, more importantly, it is also one of our family lineages. It chronicles our history, Hikune. It also traces our abilities and confirms our right as dragon riders. Come, my boy, walk with me to see my dragon with whom your father was named after. He is little more than a two day's journey walk while at his cave grounds with his mate and along the way I will tell you of how the human race was formed, rose, and fell." The pair packed for the upcoming days and nights. Gathered rations for food and drink, then set off to see Hikothe's oldest friend, his dragon, Hikarge.

As soon as they entered the main road from the estate Hikothe started in a friendly yet firm voice, "I don't suppose I can dissuade you from hearing this tale can I, young sir? The contents of this book will do one of two things, either strengthens your understanding of the world, or simply break your resolve as everything you learned and know will be uprooted. Either way, you will not be the same young boy standing in front of me." He looked at his grandson shaking his head vigorously and wearily smiled, remembering his son reacting the same way when he first showed him the book. Thus, the old Dama started with the tale of human history, as well as the history of his people and family. "Well I assume the only way to fully explain this story is to start from the absolute beginning, when the High God brought his angels to a blank land. You see son, we hear and say the word angels now because history eventually changed it, but the angels you heard about in the ancient books are, in fact, the same dragons you see now. However, immensely stronger and more gifted were those original creatures. The dragons you see now are the descendants of those 'angels'. Rynesch, the Sky Queen was the largest and first dragon put on this planet. He placed her here and asked what she saw. He wanted to see if she thought this land had potential to do more than support mere growth for her. In honesty, she could not see it at first, but the High God promised it would be a grand place for his first creations so long as they protected and proctored over it. And then something similar to the creation story you read about previously in my old study took place. Though not as simple as it was stated in that old leather bound book. "First He scorched the planet for hours so he could have a clean canvass to do his best for his dragon angels. He took the elements of the planet to enhance his dragons in ways they never dreamed. He told Rynesch, that they would use the special powers to govern the earth, their new home. The High God took the steam flowing upwards from the cooked ground, gathered it, and made a storm to course over the earth, removing the debris of his burnt wreckage. The entirety of it was sucked upwards to the heavens and created a barrier, trapping in the air we now breathe. He then pulled away the strong wind and absorbed the giant storm. He then condensed it and placed the rampant power in Rynesch's soul. She blasted and flipped, twirled and stretched. It felt like the best part of her spirit grew a hundred times. She looked at the sky with new eyes. With even clearer vision she could see miles ahead on this new planet that she was to lord over. Simple details as to which way the wind blew a pebble became easily noticed. She could smell the flamed soil, the nutrient rich earth beneath it, and even the hot boiling lava below that. She was overjoyed with the new sensations. She then flew up to meet with the High God as he smiled at her."

"What else is in store for me and my new world, father?" asked Rynesch.

"Well, my dearest dragon, now you will need one that can serve you with not only power, but honor and wisdom. Do you have anyone in mind that can fulfill this, one of the greatest tasks I ask? They will be the champion of this planet, for not only dragons, but whoever comes next," asked the High God.

"I do know such the soul, and he has earned my complete trust and confidence in his abilities to fulfill this task. He is my third in command, Sherygha. As trusting and wise as myself, but not as lazy as my second in command, I am wholly confident he will be perfect for this job, as well as deserving of this pleasure. That is, if you see fit my highness."

"I know him well. We have had many talks and is an excellent choice," remarked the High God. He called down Sherygha from the heavens. And while the gigantic dragon descended down, wings gliding on the newly formed sky, he saw the High God put a triple sized mountain of ice, larger than that he had ever seen at his original home, on the opposite ends of the scorching planet. "Sub-captain Sherygha, you have been promoted this day to the status of Captain. You will make this new land your home. It is your duty to govern over it under Rynesch as her second in command. You are strong, honorable, and wise. But in this new place you will need more than the power you already possess. As I gave her the power of the storm winds, I will also give elements of this planet to you. However, as the enforcer you will hold two elements, to ensure you stay the strongest of this world. Use the powers I bestow upon you to govern wisely." Then the High God pulled a source from the

Ice Mountains, still cooling the scorched planet, and then, from the lava resonating deep within the earth, the High God pulled up a portion of the boiling red liquid within and placed both together. He spun the balls of energy until they mingled and placed it in Sherygha. Loudly he proclaimed, so the planet itself would know, just as the ones watching above in the heavens, "This is my insurance. He is the one that will do what is just and keep balance and order in this new world. I place in him, two opposites so that he never forgets the battle of the soul that takes place when forged with power. He is the strongest and wisest amongst you. Trust his judgment, as have I."

The ice melted down and steadily flooded the still simmering earth. Quickly, large portions of the ground below soaked up new water. Cracks, holes and crevices filled, delegating the water to various areas of the land mass. Looking to the sky, he wiped his eyes and blew hard into his graceful hands. Darkness overcame the land. He created the night to let the ground cool.

The next morning, the High God entered the atmosphere with his two ruling dragons. He outstretched his fingers and all manner of plants grew from the lava rich soil. He put all the herbage needed for the earth, the dragons, and its future inhabitants to live and thrive. He then decreed to all the dragons that were awarded safe passage that in addition to the celestial power they were given at creation, they would inherit traits from an element of the new world as they passed through the archway connecting the heavens and their new home. As the new gift of power was from the elements he used to make the planet, the powers were Wind, Fire, Ice, Earth, Water and Lightning. Thus, as the dragons entered this atmosphere they all felt the surge of power, much like Rynesch, granted to them from the generous High God. He looked at them with love as they entered. He was pleased he created a world for his best creations, yet, he realized they still needed more. With this great power, so was their hunger. So the High God created the animals, big and small. He filled the waters with fish to swim and then the sky with birds to fly alongside the heavenly creatures. As the day progressed, he retreated home, leaving the dragons to eat and explore their new home.

"Now Hikune, this is where the books you have read in the past and the old book you hold now truly differ," warned Hikothe. "It was not the next day that the High God created man like it said in the other books. Instead, he waited. He wanted all the creatures of the new earth to know that dragons were the dominant species. Some animals died out. You know them as dinosaurs. Many were eaten, or were caught between rivaling dragons. But many also evolved to the animals you read about in other books. Some are still around today, continuously evolving as we do. This time period lasted a few thousand years. It is the only period of history, before time knew humans on this world. Nevertheless, the High God was about to change all of that, and with that, changed history forever, for not only dragons, but the human race and the earth as well."

THE LAST SPECIES

"Rynesch, Sherygha, the time has come for me to finish the planet. The last phase will begin now, thus your hardest task. I allowed for you and the dragons to grow on this planet. I wanted your species to learn your abilities thoroughly for this reason. I will be adding a new species to the Earth. They will all have different aspects to them. Thus will grow and thrive in different climates so they will have room to move and multiply on this earth. They will not be as wise as you dragons and will need your guidance. Watch over them and keep them safe, for like the dragons, they will also be granted with souls. But like any soul, it can be loving and pure, or malevolent and dark. Nevertheless, you must watch them closely, while still allowing them to grow as a species. They shall be forged in various versions of my own image and from the powers that I used when creating this world. For that reason, they will be your companions of this world to share." And with that the High God moved away to a plain land with a small lake set a few miles before a mountain where three dragons, two born of the earth, lay. He pulled a handful of leaves off a red plant with dark golden roots that grew wild and rapidly around the lake's edge. He whispered to the bright red leaves and let them blow with the wind. Upon their landing appeared bodies in lieu of the red leaves. Seven bodies, four male, three female, and all grown to an adult age so they would be able to work the land. The

High God had set forth to begin this new era on Earth, and from the tall plant leaves they were named after, he created the first of the new species, the Norfex.Very common are the physical traits of the Norfex. They are a race of medium height and build. They all had brown eyes, but like the tall beautiful plants before them they were gifted with long red hair. Yet as a contrast to the hair, they have golden brown skin, mimicking the root of the Norfex plant thus protecting from the direct sunlight. The High God then placed ten full families, set in various stages of life. He called privately away and then spoke to the seven created, but also the elders of the families and told them his will to multiply the Earth and grow as a species. He informed them that the dragons would watch over them and would guide them to reaching their highest potential. It was the elder species' world first, but the youngest of all his creations would dwell alongside them on this paradise.

The elders of the families returned to the grass mounds they came from and asked the dragons to show them how to build shelter. The three dragons did, and in return, were groomed and allowed to feast with them. They rejoiced in the fact that in their first day of creation they had berries to eat and pieces of meat they came to know as fish, however, more than anything they were happy for the company. These few dozen people were the first and only of their species in the entire world. The dragons spoke to them, telling them stories of their history and how the world came to be. Then they made the first seven members of the newly created Norfex the governing body and showed them the difference between the edible plants and animals. And once they were too tired to keep moving, the Norfex members returned to the mud enclosures made by the three dragons and slept deeply. The day had been exhausting and the first members of the dual legged species still had much to learn tomorrow.

Yet, in another part of the world the High God took two nearby dragons into a cave. He looked around at the hard stone and natural ores and using his mind, pulled up an old man from its properties. He was very short and stout. His strength already set into his frame to work this solid type land. He gave him broad fingers and large hands. With that he furnished a greater nose to breathe in large amounts of the stifled atmosphere to keep air flowing in his compact body. He put life into the man and told him that he was an Uckleet, forged from the cave they were standing in, and his race would work the mines and caves to bring precious metals and ores up to the surface. So it was said, and such it became. He gave the Uckleet man a staff of jewels and gold, with various rings, and bracelets on his neck and fingers, though the man did not understand the meaning at the time. He was then told that he should work with the dragons to make a life for him and his family. And at that mention, a young Uckleet woman with child walked out of the shadows and bowed before the newly awakened man. As the High God was walking away he motioned to his left and right, and eight other families appeared, four to each side. Along with the eight families, thirteen other members aroused from the free lying stones. All of the same general Uckleet build and make. All of them had hazel eyes, rosy skin and light brown hair.

A red male dragon with onyx tint and edging corralled the Uckleet members and began explaining the world to them. The dragon insisted that they follow a high monarchy structure as that was how most animals of the world functioned, and since the High God already made one richer than the rest, he should be their ruler. The others agreed to the logic and all kneeled as the dragon proposed, to show respect to their new leader. They then followed the dragons deeper into the caves to learn the trade that would eventually become the basis of their life. The dragons spoke to them of different subjects and they learned much from them. And as a favor to the High God and proud of the fast learning race, the red dragon flew out the cave to bring back fresh game for the new species to eat.

Sensing their hunger and his cunning over the group, the other dragon, a green and pearl, told them that if they did not desire to wait, they could simply eat the snails and wonderful creatures of the cave and would be equally happy. Many of the Uckleet did as the dragon offered and ate the snails and insects he gave them. He happily caught and fed them a multitude of roaches and cave slugs to try filling the miniature people. Thus, when the red dragon returned, many were full from the small disgusting and slimy creatures. Then as soon as the red dragon dropped the fresh caught bull to check on the health of the new sentient beings on earth, the green dragon silently devoured half the animal without offering any of the newcomers, even the ones still hungry, a morsel. When they realized his treachery, the green grabbed the second half of the beast and fled the cave before they, or the red male could attack him. Such was the introduction to the planet Earth for the Uckleet. They learned a very harsh reality within hours of breathing the cave's air. Some beings would help, while others would trick, so they would have to all stick together as they grow to ensure nobody else takes advantage of them so blatantly ever again.

On the other side of the vast continent, a large brown dragon that crossed through the heavenly arc cleared an opening in the forest for the High God. Getting tired from using massive amounts of his energy and power to create life again, the High God made the final group of the species for the day. He took the root of a Mylare tree in his hand and spoke directly to it while running his other hand over the dangling portion. Instantly, the tree bore fruit. The brown dragon with emerald accents that favored the forest regions most watched his creator in action once again. It seemed the fruit the tree bore were quickly taking shape as they elongated to a massive cocoon. There also appeared to be a bounty of the new fruit. The High God shone a blinding light from his eyes on the tree. He smiled and placed both of his hands on the dragon's crest, sending him a warming sensation. He patted the large brown one last time and then departed.

Slowly and steadily the cocoons began to open one after the other, like the opening of a portal into a new world and new reality. More and more hands, heads and feet emerged from the enchanted tree. They all eventually released themselves from the cocoon and migrated towards the majestic dragon standing before them.

"I am not here to hurt you, new people created of the forest. I have a message from our creator, the High God, who returned home, too weak to continue today. He told me you are a new race of specie on this planet we call earth. You are the Mylare, grown and designed from the tree you departed from. I came through the heaven arc long ago and have lived many years, thus

I am your guide to prosperity. I love the trees and the forest, thus I have personally been chosen to help you understand its ways so you may function within its limits and thrive. Please do not fear me, for I mean you no harm. Yet also be warned, dear creatures. Do not cross me, or I will not hesitate to devour you. I look forward to knowing each of you well.

"I was left with a small list about who you are to assist me in your guidance. First, you are the tallest of all the races he has created. This is to better gather the fruits of the day. Though with this height, you will lack some strength, but where you lack strength, He has given you incredible speed and the longest spans of life of your species. So you can hunt a prey, or outrun an enemy. Yes, my new friends, you will soon learn, the forest is full of enemies."

The brown and emerald dragon looked out at his crowd, which seemed to have gotten even larger than when he first began speaking. The ones in the front were pale with red eyes. Their hair was a mixture of white and green like the cocoons they just broke free of. Just as the High God said, their ears were narrow towards the top, allowing them to channel the sounds of the jungle more acutely than any other race as well. Although, as he looked around, he noticed towards the back that the small area of more shaded cocoons were producing members with a slight tint to the pale skin of the ones that were grown in the light. They also wore different facial expressions and multicolored strands of hair mixed with the white opposed to the normal green. Not exactly sure what to make of the difference, he decided to keep watch more closely than he had thought, but say nothing about it now.

The brown dragon brought back a very large male deer and breathed fire to burn it. The Mylare looked in awe at the bright spectacle. They were astounded at the heat that emanated from the charring object. And to add another sense to be awakened, the smell was absolutely salivating, though they were unsure why. Suddenly, a score of the darker Mylare from the back lunged forward and grabbed the cooking meat. In immediate response, all of the Mylare became perfectly aware of what was in front of them. In a mad rush all the Mylare were scrambling to receive a piece of the fantastic piece of sultry meat. The dragon hastened towards the group, grabbed the chunk of meat he brought and took to the sky. He tore off two legs and dropped them for the new people to eat. When they did that, he dropped two more off and ordered the ones who already ate to retreat to the other side of the tree to drink from the water of the Claupine River. As the second group was eating, the dragon noticed three of the darker Mylare attacking others for more food, even though everyone had not yet eaten. The emerald edged dragon placed the rest of the kill on a sturdy branch, dove forward and caught one of the dark Mylare with white and burnt orange hair by the waist in his massive front claws. Without hesitation he bit off the dark Mylare's head, spit it to a patch of weeds near the river's edge and with a flick of his neck, ate the body of the Mylare whole. He looked at the other Dark Mylare and let out a deep stern growl. It was a warning from before, 'do not cross me, or I will surely devour you'. Most of the Dark Mylare retreated into the forest, leaving the pale Mylare to offer praises for his protection. The big dragon continued to teach the new people as promised. Though this time, there were only a handful of dark Mylare present to learn. The two separate Mylare factions were never able to fully rejoin each other that day, ultimately setting the stage for a lifetime of war and discontent between the brothering Mylare clans.

The High God returned after waiting two hundred and fifty years. He wanted to allow the races he already placed on the planet to grow and mature. He anticipated that after a few generations and the dragons' guidance, order and prosperity would be established within the races. Laws and a governing body would be set and the second phase of the species could be introduced. Alas, such was not the case. The dragons that were supposed to be helping the young species either betrayed them, or taught them basic survival skills, but not wisdom and a better logic. Though a small hierarchy had been set amongst the groups, so did rivalry. There was little expansion and growth between the races since each race held primarily to themselves.

So the High God slightly altered the plans he had for the new generation of the species he copied in his images. He needed a people that would be able to help, coexist, and love their keepers, his first species, and the 'angel' dragons. People that would not be afraid to venture more than a few miles and that could learn and teach.

Immediately the High God went to the north of the land. He was passing a range of mountains where settlements of the Norfex had begun to spring up with more speed than either of the other two races. He noticed they also used stones from the mountain, meaning they had met and bartered with the Uckleet dwelling near them. With a feeling of delight at the small growth in the right direction, he waved his hands over what seemed like two large community farms. Right before the eyes of the Norfex communities a sudden overabundance became of the crops. There were enough crops to store in the settlements and to trade with the other Norfex communities that had spread when the various elders decided to disperse for their own lands or even the Uckleet if they desired.

After seeing the joy of his youngest species, he left for the colder climate of the north. There, he called upon a young ice dragon of about four years old that he saw having a meal. He demanded that this dragon, dark blue with copper edges, show the people he will be creating how to more than survive, but live and thrive as the dragons do. Softly the High God settled on an open patch of land that was vast. It was not very green due to the cold soil, but still supported life. Thus larger animals like bison and deer were sparse, but there was an easy, albeit long road going south east and leading into the mountains where the Uckleet originated. And to the west, though shorter, was a direct road to some settlements at the base of the Claupine River. Both roads, if taken to completion, would also eventually lead this new race to settlements of the nomadic Norfex.

This must be the best place to offer the new race growth. Small rocks could form homes, and the small stream flowing down from the ice miles ahead offered many different fish to eat and fresh water to drink. And there was an abundance of small animals for food and clothes since it had little interference from the dragons and other houmans.

Thus, the High God pulled over a boulder of the large, strong arfaet rock from under the icy ground. He molded a large man, even larger than the broad Norfex, to be able to move the rocks and land of this region. He gave him slate skin like the rocks they derived from. The eyes were already a hue of blue-grey, thus the High God left them as they were, so they would be able to see clearer in the dreary climate of the north. And so they would have a natural ability to find each other, he extracted the light color of an inedible and poisonous plant near the new site and gave him blonde hair. He touched the rock hand and whispered into his stony ear. Suddenly the rock began to crack and break into pieces as the High God moved away. As the chips of arfaet rock fell away, the solid body of the Arfaet man appeared. He looked upon his new creation and saw strength in him as he wanted, but not the gentleness of the nature of the youngest species. Thus he gathered the pieces of rock that had shelled the new man, and put them back together. Then he clasped his hands tightly and the rock began to grind into each other and slightly shift. The broad shoulders and hard jawline were now smoother. The hands and feet were smaller and more delicate. The High God then blew over the figure and refined it, making it smooth. She breathed. The rocks, as was with the man, fell away. This woman would be a vast difference in shape than the figure standing next to her, looking in astonishment at the power of his creator and the gentle structure of his work. In comparison she was smaller like a Norfex, but stronger and bigger still than any other of the female versions of the races.

"I am the High God" he bellowed from across the distance. "This is an ice dragon, here to watch over you, and teach you how to live and thrive. This land is not the most hospitable, but if you work hard it can support you. And later, as you venture further south, you will find other types of races much like yourself, though they are older and different. Like you, they are fitted for the environment they inhabit. Use my knowledge, and my servant. Let him guide you to becoming a prosperous race. Create trade and place roads with them, for the growth of one, will be the growth of the other. And with that in your minds, I will create thirty more like you from the same rock as you. Guide them, your people well." He turned towards the giant boulders and thrust his hands towards them. Calling them forth, the boulders rolled to the front of their master. He drove his hands into the surface, as they rippled like a pond. He then began to move his hands in circular motions. He moved his arms faster and faster, hands still submerged. Once he finished, he retracted his hands and moved back to the cave wall. Approving his work, he sighed and smiled. The rock fell away, as it had with the first two, and thirty individuals, fifteen males and females ventured forward as if being pulled. He told them to trust the two before them and follow their example. And with that being said the High God patted the young ice dragon, elevated to the sky and ventured south east.

The blue ice dragon, not at all pleased with being disturbed by his father's creator leapt upon the firstly created Arfaet, snarling above his face. He thought about eating him for a moment, then thought about the repercussions he may incur from older dragons that were created by the High God, especially the black one named Sherygha that his father warned about. He backed off the man and helped him up. Then unexpectedly he bit the man on his arm. Not enough to tear it off, but still enough to forever leave the wound marks. The blue ice dragon branded the man in defiance of the High God. The original Arfaet man screamed in agony, as it was the first time experiencing pain. The dragon walked towards him again as the man kept trying to back away. Then the dragon breathed his power over the wounded arm, and quickly it began the process of healing.

"I will show you how to not only survive, but also thrive" yelled the blue and copper dragon to the new people on earth. "I will make sure you understand pain. If you know pain, you will understand joy. If you have nothing, like you do now, you will revel in having plenty. And believe me, I will truly show you how."

The dragon helped teach them how to build a sparse, rickety shelter of the loose rocks and cold mud that was there. Then after having the people pour water over the shelters he used his power and froze them so they would last the nights to come. He showed them a sharp edge of a rock that was near them and told them to hunt for food after a brief demonstration. The men all went for the hunting experience. The women stayed and finished making the shelters. However when the men were almost back, having caught two small rodents of the area and a fair sized fish, they saw the ice dragon fly above them towards the camp site. When they finally arrived, they saw the same dragon thrashing about, breaking the very shelters he had them create. He then took the food they caught and told them to do everything again. He laughed at them and said if they wanted to gain anything, they were to do it or take it for themselves. Then he attacked each of them, jumping around from one to another as they ran around the camp looking for any kind of hiding place. He only bit down hard enough to leave two canine imprints into their arms, much like he did the first one of their race, but offering less injury, though this time he did not heal them at all. Then he took all the food they hunted and ate it in front of them. Hungry, wounded, exhausted, and angry at their treatment after the ordeal, they huddled together for the night.

After nearly an hour of waiting for the dragon to unleash more of his fury the first Arfaet man stood up, looked at his people that the High God gave him to instruct and protect. Then he peered down at the marks on his now healed arm, thinking about all that transpired in his first day. He was lost, and did not know what to do. The dragon's voice sounded in his throbbing head, 'I will make sure you understand pain.' Then abruptly he remembered his most recent words, 'if you want anything, you will have to take it.' He walked over to two other men, grabbed them by their injured arms and told them they would hunt again. He mildly looked at the dark blue and copper dragon, walked over and fell to his knees, burying his face into the cold ground. When the dragon stood above him, the first Arfaet whispered something. Leaning in to hear what the injured creature said, the man swiftly jabbed the dragon in the neck as he was to do with the fish and small animals he caught for food. Staggering and furious, the dragon wanted to jump upon the broad man, but the pain in his neck was too much to tolerate and fight. Instead he dashed toward the huddle, grabbed one of the other hunters with his powerful hind claws and launched himself into the air with powerful wing strokes. He tried turning his head to launch an ice attack before his retreat but the injury proved to be too painful. He abandoned the cold, hungry and battered Arfaet with no shelter, food, or guidance.

The Arfaet man, weary and dazed, now understood what the dragon said. They knew pain now, but would later know joy. He left them with nothing, but they would eventually have everything. The large blue and copper dragon had been ruthless to them, and he would be the same to all outside his people. It was at that time, the original Arfaet man swore if he ever saw the blue ice dragon with copper edges again, he and his people would completely devour him.

While the Arfaet were dealing with the hard lessons of the ice dragon, the High God approached the lake he was looking for. It was a lake enchanted with his power. It neither fills from streams or rivers nor supports other bodies of water from its immense size. It instead, gets its water from the underworld tip of the northern ice caps that meet the lava. The ice caps, created by the High God's power, delve deep into the earth's crust. It melted, and then traveled upwards along a crevice. It filled the lake, full of not only water, but also mystical properties. Many dragons, as he learned, use it to rejuvenate themselves and fill their power sacs again. The fish inside are therefore also enchanted and can do many wonders, like heal wounds or give a boost of energy to the creature that feasts upon them.

The High God first sat at the lake edge and drank a few handfuls of the water. He then dipped his head in and filled on its water and power. He would use the same power to create his next race. Gathering a few gallons of its water, he swirled it about over the land in front of him. Then he reached out, found a large fish and bled it. Then he brought a large bird and lizard, and did the same. He mixed the blood of the animals with the water and poured in into a mountainous ant hill. As the ants scattered he killed the kings and the queen, as to ensure a race of mutant ants were not created. Then once a score of ants had reached a distance, he blew over them. Immediately the ants turned into a giant gelled substance, much like the cocoons of the Mylare. He slowly uplifted his hands and pulled out the water he first poured into the ant hill and poured it over the colony of cocoons. Then he spoke to them. "I am your creator. I am giving you a small portion of my power, so you can assist your species in becoming compatible with the dragons that fly above you, swim with you and walk among you. Being mixed with different animal blood and of my most sacred waters, you are undeniably special to this world. Cater to it. Use your powers to heal it. Protect it and protect yourselves from any and all harm. Know that knowledge is the only way to use your powers wisely. It can be a great asset, but also a great curse." The High God summoned Sherygha and then spoke to him. "My wonderful friend, these are the greatest of my newest beings. They have power like dragons, though much more limited. I beg you, please expel your knowledge so that they will not stray and use their essence for evil purposes. They do not know the temptation that will bestow them to turn to darkness. You are the wisest of the dragons, and after many talks with me, have learned more. Do your best to teach them. I trust you with this over all else, so they will know how to wield their power and do not destroy my creation and your home, this planet earth."

The cocoons began ripping open. The grand dragon

walked over to see the new experience. He looked back, saw his creator and friend smiling at his newest creation, and nodded in agreement to his request. With that nod, the High God drank one more time of the enchanted lake, and stored some for later. He then shrouded himself in a cloud and ascended into the sky and out of the dragon's sight.

Sherygha observed the little grey hands reaching out and pulling apart their encasings. He counted up to forty seven of the cocoons, but he did not assist them in attaining their liberty. If they were to justly learn the world, and who they are, they would need to pass this first test without his help. The ones that did come out looked around and began to huddle in the water. Some ventured out a little further, but before they could get deep enough to drown he froze an arc into to watery mass, enclosing the new race and forcing them to pay attention to him while they wait on their brethren.

"Why have you trapped us in here" demanded one of the new people. Sherygha could feel the power simmering in him. And that feeling was spreading amongst the captured people. The giant dragon knew that if he did not do something soon, the new mortal would do something foolish, like attack a dragon. And if he attacked the dragon, he would have to die, and the people, new into the world, would never trust him to teach them how to prosper as the High God expected. So he roared. Not a small roar that scares out a few animals so he can chase and eat them while the blood was still hot. No, this was the loud, boisterous roar of an entity that could destroy mountains if pushed too far. It was a roar that all within earshot would tremble with fear from being in the same area as a being of superior existence, and knowing its intentions.

"I am not your enemy, fair creatures," spoke the dragon. He looked out at grey bodies with purple eyes and black hair and wondered what creature had the High God created this time. Physically they looked similar to the High God in a way, but like all the other members of this newest species, they were also different. "The one talking to you while slumbering was our creator. I am a dragon, and the strongest of the land. And after many, many talks and lessons with the High God I am also the wisest. He has entrusted me to rearing you into becoming productive and flourishing members of this world."

As he hovered over them, he counted thirty eight members of the new race, enhanced with the gifted properties of the lake, looking up at him. He knew this point in time would not be the best time to tell them they were more gifted than the rest of the races in world, minus the dragons themselves. Knowing all too well where he was, he told them to follow him. Unbeknownst to the community below, in the center of the enormous lake were three large islands, so close they seemed one massive property island. Sherygha decided this would be their home land. So as they grow, they can add to the land and if anyone should get too out of hand with the power usage, the lake would absorb it back into itself before it reaches the main land. Then, once they have learned how to control the power within, they will be able to reach out on their own and explore the land of Choi as well as the other races of their young species. Sherygha told the group to climb aboard the ice shelf he created earlier. Then he formed a bridge leading to the island.

The island was not, by any means close, but the dragon herded the thirty eight members along anyway.

He knew they were strong, but the voyage would take three days by foot, and they needed get there as soon as possible so they could rest safely, and then learn what he had to teach them. As they, the populace and the large dragon, walked towards their new home he spoke of the world. Of the other races and how they developed. Of the dragons and their elemental powers he spoke more in depth. The people were very inquisitive. It was the first race the old dragon spoke with of this new Earth species and enjoyed it. He was in a good mood and the sun was setting, reflecting hues of red and orange against their grey skin. He told them they would make camp for a few hours to eat and rest. Then he shot into the sky. He did a loop and spread his massive wings wide. Though he did not mean to, he sent chills of fear to the people below. Seeing him in such a bold posture reminded them of the roar earlier. He collapsed his wings and darted down toward the group on the ice bridge. They huddled together in fear as he expected, yet right before he crashed into the water, he spit out an oily fire along the edge of the bridge. Seeing fire for the first time, but hearing about its properties from the dragon earlier, the people were perplexed. They were told dragons were awarded one planetary element to rule the world with. However, this towering dragon Sherygha, who they previously believed was of ice, easily and quite effectively used fire also.

"Who are you, dragon," asked one of the new grey men with alarm in his eyes. "Why can you control two elements?"

The dragon swung his body low against the air current of the tide, twirled upward, and dove into the water. He saw a very large fish. One that was capable of feeding all of the people on the bridge and appeasing a tired dragon. It was grey with two black stripes on each side of its spine. Simultaneously he noticed the scales toward the back had a purple hue. He spread his massive slightly webbed claws and darted underwater towards the large fish. Before it could react to the giant black dragon, it was caught between its expansive jaws and muscular arms. He pushed up from his hind legs until he broke the water's surface, and then let his colossal wings lift him and the stunned fish out of the water and onto the bridge. The herd had migrated over to the fire to warm themselves. They were now running to the spectacle of seeing how formidable and graceful their dragon truly was. He dropped the large fish. Used a digit of his front claw and cut out a large piece of the flesh. He placed it on the ice and breathed fire over it, this time omitting the oily saliva with it. He told everyone to take a piece of the cooked fish. They all did as was told and immediately they began changing. Many looked stronger and healthier. Others began to slightly glow in the setting sun. The hair on one female grew twice its length. Sherygha smiled and laughed to himself. He saw this was the trigger. Like the rock of the Arfaet, the cave surface of the Uckleet, the plant of the Norfex and the tree of the Mylare, he used a piece of this world to make them. Thus he told them as such and why this particular fish created such reactions. Sherygha declared "As I have seen you this day, grow with the eating of the fish I brought, I now know your origins. You, like your species will follow and be named by this. From this moment until eternity, you, your children, and your children's grand-children shall be the race known as the Ormaques." Sherygha picked up the fish by the tail, showing the entire parties present what it looked like, and how they mimicked it. When the action had been understood by the mass, he flew ahead a good bit and in peace ate the fish in its entirety. He still had the wall of fire on one side and decided to create another on the other. It would warm the bridge inhabitants for the next few hours while they slept, and kept away anyone looking for a free meal. Then the enormous dragon lay down, covering himself with his wings, and slept.

Sherygha awakened two hours later to a crashing sound. He quickly turned around to see a dragon had braved through his barrier and was gaining his footing again. The Ormaques were all scrambling towards him, frenzied and in hopes of getting away from this new intruding dragon. Sherygha stood and roared to alarm the smaller dragon of his presence, but the white dragon just laughed and dashed toward one female that fell on the ice. He pinned her down and bit off half her torso, swallowing the top half of her body. He was reaching down for the second half when he felt his neck pressed against the ice under him. He looked up and for the first time realized who he was fighting. In a panic he swiped at the black dragon in hopes of freeing his neck. However, enraged at the insolence of the younger dragon and the fact that he killed two people when he crashed through the ice and another woman in an attempt to eat her, Sherygha would not be assuaged. He whipped his tail around and struck the smaller dragon against the right hind leg. Using his front claws he opened the dragon along the spine, spewing scales and blood in all directions. The pain shook through the small dragon and he wrenched himself free, losing chunks of flesh in the process. He blasted Sherygha with a ball of earth and rock then haphazardly took to the sky. The irate black dragon darted to the sky in chase. He quickly overtook the smaller white dragon. The two dragons, twirled around in battle, shooting earth against ice. Wings were beating, and roars were sounding. Sherygha was beating and ripping at his enemy while the little one tried all he could to fight back and possibly escape. Winning was never an option. Straining to gain the higher altitude the dragon turned tightly and beat his wings as hard as he could with the horrible back injury. Success! The large dragon had released his grip finally. The smaller white dragon sought emotional reward for not backing down to the captain of dragons. The effort, however, was futile. Sherygha grabbed the dragon by the waist and base of his tail, and blasted him with a ball of fire and ice that not only left a large hole in his body, but left his innards steaming and searing. He dropped the limp body of the dead dragon into the waters of the lake to let the aquatic creatures eat what was left of the thick muscular meat. However, as he looked down, he was astonished. In a mad surge, there was half of the Ormaque populace swimming towards the slowly sinking dragon. Yet that was only the smallest portion of the astounding sight. Because right before his eyes, the ones swimming to consume the dragon were of normal upper bodies, but completely fish below, grey and purple like the one they were derived after. He observed the spectacle with inquiry. Never before had Sherygha seen such a sight. It was like nothing he had ever heard of before. They were half man, and half fish, working as one whole mind and body, and moving, swiftly to devour the dragon that attacked them. In only a few seconds, the group approached the dead dragon and began consuming it. They were getting stronger by the minute, and the power in them was taking control in ways he never expected. And with a splash, the second group also turned into the creatures their empowered race created, and went to meet them. It became a crazed feeding ground, eating not only the cooked meat from the fire of the killing blast, but soon the raw meat of the white and emerald dragon as well. One by one, after eating their fill, the members of the intriguing race left and returned to the ice shelf. The weird entity would sit on the shelf, and in a glimmer, turn their tails into legs and feet again. Then walk upright, fixing their sharp toothed back to the normalcy of their species. Sherygha was stunned to silence, and what's more, had no way to begin explaining this to the head dragon, Rynesch or their creator, the High God.

He decided they needed to reach the islands as soon as they could. So he used the new transformation of this race to his advantage. He broke the ice shelf behind him completely since it had already cracked from the intrusion. Then told them to do it again, the shape shift and meet him at the first island they reached. He then swooped down and broke the ice bridge, bringing down his tail like a hammer. "Tarry not if you desire to live, for now that you are fed and full of power, it is the best chance you have to reach it before tiring and being taking by the water. To answer your earlier question my new friends, like I previously told you, my name in Sherygha. Though what I did not tell you was that I am the dragons' enforcer on this world. I am the strongest and wisest of my kind on this planet. Thus the High God deemed me with two separate powers, the opposites of fire and ice, to remember that in order to properly utilize power there must first be balance. That is why I am your instructor of this new world of ours. You will need not only my wisdom, but my actual practice of this gift, if you want to truly control who you will become." Then Sherygha launched into the sky and steadily flew towards the island. He only spared a single glance back, but when he saw the hurried swimming of a multitude, grey with purple eyes, he steeled his will and advanced to the future home of the Ormaques, thus the future of his entire world.

The High God hovered above the world in thought. He needed a race that would think. They would be a race that was not of the earth and gained prosperity not by physicality or force, but primarily by intellect. He returned home for what was to be a night. However that was not the case.

The High God returned from the timeless land one hundred and eighty-five years later and then decided to travel south; for he felt he had the perfect position for their creation. It was the rocky plains just above a fertile span of earth and edged a small forest, now being slightly occupied by a few families of the pale and dark Mylare. First he summoned his chief dragon, Rynesch, and then he took out the water he retrieved from the powered lake in which he created the Ormaque race from. He shook it furiously and then with the palms of his hand made it steam and create a cloud. He took the cloud and positioned it right between the end of the slightly rocky desert and the grass of the more fertile land leading to the forest on the east. Then he clenched his hand into a fist and brought it down like a hammer against his other hand. The cloud made of the enraptured water broke and just as suddenly rained down on that one ration of land it was positioned. A strong wind blew and some of the enraptured mud was pulled out of the ground. The High God collected all of the land touched by the water. He burned the ground, letting the ash fall back down to re-fertilize the soil. The steam and trace particles still in the air was again collected. Now filtered over and over, he put together, what seemed like a frivolously grainy air to the elderly dragon. He made the woman brown skinned, and her eyes, black. They needed to be the darkest hue so they would see anywhere they roamed. And with the sun setting in the distance, he gave her hair a burnt orange coloring, just brighter than rust. He made her shapelier than all the other races. She would need child bearing hips so their race would populate quickly. The High God was no longer taking chances on dragons or the planet earth to assist his favorite creation since the dragons so long ago. He was giving this race, the last of the new species he created all the abilities he wanted of it. Although he knew it would come at a price. He decided to take away high physical ability, like the Norfex, Uckleet, or Arfaet. No extra strength or height would be of the final race. He would not give them stocky arms to mine the land or power to evade and destroy. He would give them, and ensure them using the one thing he hoped the other races would have achieved, the tool of intelligence. He then pulled his fingers, lengthening the lifespan of the new creation. Intelligence, speed from such light constitution, and longevity were to defenses of the new people. Thus the High God finished forming the soft, semi-weak body and bade her to wake up. When she did, she realized she was not on the ground. He told her she was not made of earth, but because of that, she and her people would be physically weak. So to have stronger offspring, she, and the ones like her must meet the other races and mix with them. Like she will need their strengths to survive, they direly needed her intellect.

Then the High God waved his right palm across the sky, and three dozen Hufore birds flew towards them, each coming from a different direction. Thus when birds began to collide, a flurry of feathers was set loose and fell. The High God smiled when the confusion was over asked the new woman to look down on the ground. "These feathers will be your followers. Treat them kindly. Tonight I will impart to all of you as much wisdom as your brains will be able to completely understand, process, and put into practice. Much more you will learn on your own through your travels, for your race will be nomadic, never truly settling until you have seen the entire land. I am sorry to make this your burden, but it is the only way to bring the other five races out of their own darkness." Then, as he looked down again, he said "rise, in the making of your queen, Hufore." Then, all of the feathers that lay on the ground grew, and stood. They took shape and then the Hufore properties. The people of sunset colored hair, black eyes, and brown skin were all standing on the ground, looking up at the queen descended upon them like a goddess they were just meeting. She looked up and right behind her was the High God. He settled on a rock and told them it was going to be a long night of learning, for this knowledge would be the key to them surviving as a race, helping the other races to evolve and the world's future.

The High God, told Rynesch to settle behind him and listen on as well. He clapped his hands and created a thunderous sound. Everyone in audience of the High God, including the large old dragon, closed their eyes to the sound. When they opened them, portions of food made up of various meats, herbs and fruits were in front of them. He touched his hand to his forehead and pouches filled with sweet water appeared as well. He asked everyone to enjoy their meals while he started giving them the knowledge they would need to first, outsmart their enemies, then the necessary information needed to change the way people thought and gained better logic.

It would prove to be a very long night. Making them already smarter than the other races, they were much more inquisitive and asked questions of 'how' and 'why'. This pleased the High God for it showed that the brain was processing the information and not just simply retaining it. And when dawn came, they were still conversing with the High God. They learned about the other origins and customs of the five races, and the dragons. They learned many plants and animals of this area and others; how to fetch fresh water and make pouches to hold it. He and Rynesch taught them how to hunt by setting traps as well as making small hunting parties and attacking the animals and fish head on with sharpened rocks and spears of wood. He told them to learn patterns amongst all beings, for once you learn the pattern and habit of the object, you will quickly know how to overcome or use it. The Hufore people spent the morning listening, and the afternoon putting it into practice. Anytime one Hufore member would get tired or hungry, a morsel of food would appear, and after consuming it, would be suddenly energized for hours.

After the sunset of the third day, the High God looked around at the settlement that was taking shape. The diversely styled shelters would last a few months, as they wanted. It would let them train, reproduce, and learn life for a while. The varying styles showed the ability to operate the land they would be residing in to still have a simple comfortable living. They did not know all of the land, but their intellect was high, and they could do one thing better than any other race he created, adapt. It was true the Norfex were also highly nomadic, but they still only settled and traveled to regions similar to the one they were birthed. So pleased with this creation was the High God, that he bade them to bring the baskets and water casks they created earlier in the day. He told them all of how proud he was, and in return would award their hard work. As a result, he looked to their right and the wild grass became a plot of tilled land, green, lush, and ready for harvest. Small rocks that were lying around became varying piles of seeds for them to plant after this crop reaping. A few fist sized rocks turned to fruits the population had yet to taste or discover. Then he, the High God, smiled and clapped his hands again, though this time it was not deafening like that of the first night. On the contrary, it was completely silent. Suddenly the baskets they were holding filled with breads, meats, herbs and edible greens. And as a last reward he snapped, causing the casks to fill with the sweet water they had the very first evening of creation. It was the High Gods love, preparation, and satisfaction with this last race he placed upon the earth that allowed him to ascend once more. Before reaching the channel at the border separating the heavens from the earth, he told Rynesch his last wish. "Rynesch, the very first of my first creations, you have been awarded this land. Watch them and guide them into an affluent future. Trust your judgment, and trust that of your captain, Sherygha. Try to help the new creatures I created as best you can, but remember, they must walk their own paths, as all my creatures do. I love you dear friend."

The High God reached out to touch the dragon he created so many millenniums ago. Though, when he created the beings, time did not move. He gave them scales so that light and water would glean off their skin as well as protect from dangers. He gave them varying hues of scale and shape of horns so they would know individuality and their ancestry. He carved the hands and feet into claws so they could dig, grapple, slice and pierce without minimal effort. He added a long, serpentine tail for balance and to be an extra defense mechanism for itself. Acute vision, hearing, and smell for hunting. Then, so they would know physical freedom, wings of grandeur, so they, his first creations may take to flight and experience the air above. In this new world, where time is no longer frozen, they have power from the planet to better protect themselves and yet will not age, though their lifespan in this paradise could possibly surpass the millenniums they spent with him. The High God became solemn.

He grabbed her by the large horn protruding from her nose and sent a warm feeling into her being. He then lifted his hand and thought about Sherygha, all while opening a small portal. A reddish purple haze accrued in the sky, yet was flowing like a river. It had a majestic feel. Becoming somewhat translucent, the duo could see the giant dragon was sleeping. So the High God touched his closest friend with a feeling of love and warmth through the gap in time and space to reach him as a memory when he woke from what seemed a well-deserved slumber. "I love you too old friend. I'm sorry there will be no more conversing between us. Protect this world like you protected mine. The world where time does not move, and my retirement" the High God released his hold on his dragons, and covered himself in a cloud like he did many times before. Though, this time the cloud was dim and heavy with sadness. The cloud carried him up through the sky and into the arc portal leading to his home, a timeless land holding his silver palace with sapphire tint and accents, for which he colored his first creation. The High God spared one last glimpse of the earth before closing the gate for what he hoped would be the last time. Leaving for retirement, he knew that if he ever returned it would be to destroy the planet, and everything on it.

THE YEARS OF EXPANSION

Tired and hungry, Dama Hikarge decided it was the best time for taking a break and getting a midday rest, and snack. Once the duo cleared the last hill, they found a large tree to sit under and enjoy the warm fall day. Hikarge pulled off his knapsack and took out a piece of dried meat, a wedge of bread and broke off a piece of the wrapped cheese. He saw his grandson do the same, though the meat and bread was of a different source. The grand man lowered himself slowly, trying not to fatigue himself in his older age, while young Hikune quickly sat across from him.

"I never heard of our creation like that grandfather," said Hikune quietly. Yet suddenly, full of inquisition and excitement he began speaking, "how could there have been six different races of humans? I thought we were all one race. Now I don't know who I am. Which race are we from? I hope we are big and strong like the Arfaet people; warriors, strong enough to even hurt a dragon. Or maybe we are mystical like the Ormaques! Oh how great it would be to be able to turn into a half fish and swim anywhere. I need to meet the other races. I know you have traveled more than me, but once I become a Rider, I will travel across the entire planet to meet the other races."

The old Dama laughed a hearty laugh at the pumped up boy. Interest, he decided, was the greatest thing in this world. For he now knew that his grandson would accept the truth, and could endure hearing the hardest part of the tale. For the beginning was just a preliminary introduction to the forming of the world and people. Now, he would divulge the family history, and by doing so, human history.

While they ate, a uniformed man they did not know saw them, and started in their direction. He had on a green uniform and a metal shield like any other knight. At his hip was a sword with a dragon's head and neck for the handle. The hilt looked as if a circle of flames. His helmet was pushed back showing a grim face. Deep green eyes and a hard set jaw focused on the eating pair.

"Who are you, and why are you on this road?" inquired the man as he neared Hikothe and his grandson, who was now standing. "This is my land, and you do not have permission to trespass. You can either turn around now, leaving the food, or pay a toll to cross"

Dama Hikothe saw the warrior place his hand on the elaborate handle of his blade. While his eyes were looking there, he noticed a large, healed over wound spanning the back of his hand. So he knew that this was not some petty thief, but a true soldier turned rogue.

"We mean you no harm sir. I was just taking my grandson here on a trip to visit an old family friend and we stopped under this great tree to take in a bit of food. But we don't want any trouble for either of us, so we shall simply be on our way to our destination and bid you good day." Then the old Dama added, "And be sure you know the laws of this land before you make a claim. I'm sure the village elder would not be pleased to know you are threatening the people in the village with payment for passage." And with that the old man slowly began to stand.

Infuriated by Hikothe's tone, the soldier quickly drew his blade and leapt toward the bent over man, but before he could pull his sword down a searing pain shot through his lower chest. The foreign knight, now seeing the dragon rider emblem on the glove of Dama Hikothe, knew his fetal error. He was attacking not a simple elderly man and his grandchild, but the Dama of the cloister and his grandson, the future ruler of Aimone.

In a last attempt to save his life he screamed profanities and reached for the now standing Hikothe. He tugged at the sword, lodged completely through his body, but was too weak to pull it out. "I'm sorry your majesty. The man who owned this land is dead. When I returned to ask his daughter's hand in marriage, I was informed he fell into the stream and hit his head. Unconscious and in the water, he drowned. I was to marry his daughter still, but she passed away before we could hold the ceremony only four months ago. So I claimed this land as my own and have been here since. I know it was not honorable, but I needed the food to live and money to keep the land. Please, please. Retract this blade and help me. I will be forever grateful to you dear sir."

Hikothe stared at him with a cold look in his eyes. "That is a very compelling story young man. My heart would normally feel for your doubled loss. But I travel this road often, and know the owner of this land well. His only daughter is not yet of marrying age, and all three sons are knights in my army. Thus the tale you spun is false. Rather, I believe you are living like a troll, bleeding the land without thought of consequence to what damage you create. Nevertheless I do believe you were once knight for some cloister at one point, but like the heritage of your green eyes, you are a dark soul, and I see no reason to spare your life." The large Dama slowly pulled out the sword, making the younger knight scream in agony. Then, without warning, he lifted the sword up and swung it down heavily, slicing through the bones and sinew in his neck. He then took the cape of the beheaded knight and cleaned his never failing blade and placed it back in its scabbard of black marble with gold decorations. He then told Hikune to grab the head and bury it under the giant tree. While his grandson carried out the task, he drug the limp, lifeless body down into the same stream that he claimed took the life of the land owner, took everything off of the body minus the undergarments, and put his body in the water. He then dug a deep hole a few yards away. He placed everything in an old wooden box that had probably stored food before it broke; minus the finely crafted sword. That would be the prize for surviving the attempt on his life. He dumped the box in the hole and covered it with the soil. Leaving a chain out for someone to one day find, he patted the dirt, said a prayer over the soul, and returned to the tree.

"You saw his green eyes too, didn't you?" inquired Hikune. "When I first saw him I thought he was just a strong Norfex, or maybe an Arfaet, but when he got closer I saw he had green eyes. So he must have been a descendant of the Dark Mylare, right?"

With a weak smile, Hikothe regarded his grandson. He was learning, and putting it into practice, but would soon be confused and full of more questions. "You are correct, yet you are also wrong my boy. You see, the second part of the book is timeline of sorts. Showing how our nomadic people mixed with the other races and helped them advance into the people we know today. So I know you have questions, but please, indulge an old man as we take the next leg of the journey and hold your questions. For this part of the story will be the most to take in."

With a woeful smile, Hikune nodded and packed his gear back together. Then out of respect he packed his grandfather's as well. That was when he saw the second sword and realized how swiftly and accurately his grandfather had reacted to the treacherous man. For the first time, he saw his grandfather not as simple and very wise man of salt and pepper hair, but the powerful Dama of Aimone.

Hikothe grabbed the newly acquired sword from the ground with his massive hands and began walking toward the road again. When he reached it he started with the story again. "The Hufore are our ancestors. Crafted out of almost air, we were, at least then, forced to use the strongest weapon awarded to us by the High God, intelligence. For after the High God left them, the queen knew she was in command of her people, but not entirely sure what to do. She queried Rynesch for guidance, but the enormous dragon would not stir, for she was in a state of immense sorrow. So the queen, named Zharda by the creator, decided she and her people would remain where they were until they could decide where to go.

She spent the next week making advancements to shelters they already built. She also added smaller buildings, wide and deep for storage of the crops they were blessed with. They planted the seeds for another season of crops and talked about what they should do next. Zharda guided the people for three years. In that time, they had grown and added children to the community. They continued the pattern of planting the right crops for the season, fishing from the wide stream in their little village, trapping a few larger animals, and breeding. Then one day, a man confronted the queen. She told them it was time for emissaries to leave the community they built and travel to the other races, imparting knowledge like the High God ordered. The antagonizing man explained that one day they would indeed need to expand the area they lived in, but that nobody should have to leave, regardless of what the High God told them. Roiled at his disrespect towards the man that gave them life, she quickly grabbed a sharp weapon they used to spear fish with and hurled it through the man's heart. He died instantly. The others looked at the queen with weariness. They had never seen anyone die except one by a wild animal. Quickly and fearfully they all bowed to the leader of their race. She stood and proclaimed, "I was the first of us all. I spoke with the Creator before all of you were created. Then, if you remember, we all sat in his company for three days and he taught us and told us what we were to do. He purposefully gave us all knowledge, and the wisdom to use it. To simply ignore that would only bring recourse upon us in the years to come. I told you all that first week that once we were fully prepared to migrate, we would. I will not send everyone in one direction though. I desire three volunteers to enter the forest to the east. We tried once before to contact them and they fled. Nevertheless

I also know they watch us as we gather food and herbs. Let us try again, to educate a commune of this race, the Mylare. Who else is in opposition of the High God's will?" Zharda skimmed the crowd with a scowl. When no hands or voices were raised, she continued, "then three of you will complete this task. It will be the first step to a life voyages for our people."

One man and one woman stood. They looked around for a third person, but instead of an individual volunteer, two people stood for the first trek. It was a man and wife. Taking their two year old son to the queen, they asked her to watch over him until they returned. She refused the couple, and told them another would have to shoulder that responsibility, however, she would personally provide the rations necessary for feeding the young growing mouth. With that being said, Queen Zharda looked at the dead body being removed for a moment and then returned to her large enclosure she built and added to over the past three years.

The four missionaries prepared food of salted fish and game, bread rolls and fruits. They did not know how long they would be there amongst the Mylare, so they petitioned for a few seeds to plant while in the forest as well. They each filled their water sacks and added a second, then bade the group farewell. It was the first time anyone would leave the village they created for more than a night, but it would not be the last, for as the High God commanded, they were to be nomadic by nature, and Queen Zharda was not going to resolve otherwise.

The assembly of four reached the forest on the third day as usual. They penetrated the forest in the same point as they always had. However this time, something was vastly different. The smell was not the same, yet still familiar. Migira, wife of Ghortu, realized what happened before the rest. The Mylare had moved closer the forest's edge than they realized. From what they scouted in gathering trips, there were only five families in this part of the forest. One was a Dark Mylare, the others, Pale. However, the families must have branched out, because the Hufore were only a few score in the lush green landscape and could see shelters amidst the trees.

Suddenly Ghortu, after hearing a light sound, turned to his left and saw five tall, lean Mylare standing with ragged spears of broken wood. The Mylare were staring at them, uncertain of what to think of the new intruders. Then, with a crack of a wood limb, another group of Mylare came to distantly greet them on the opposite side. They also held spears of broken wood. With a soft laugh from ahead, a tall lean Mylare man stepped forward. He cleared his throat then began, "you are people from outside the green land, am I correct? But you do not have the same tools as before, and have come farther down path then before. Why have you come to our community? Have you grouped with our dark Mylare brethren?" After a moment of silent response, and feeling the anxiousness rising in the other race, Bugt, the single male, spoke in answer. "We have not come with connection to anyone but ourselves. We look different, my friends because are not the gatherers. We are emissaries of the queen, Zharda, and we are here to offer our knowledge to your people."

The tall Mylare man walked briskly to the corralled group. He peered into Bugt's eyes for a moment with a furrow in his brows, then turned and spit on the ground ahead of them. Remembering what the dragon told them during that first nights conversation, Migira spit on the ground also. During the *Great Discussion*, as it has now become referred among the Hufore, Rynesch spoke of the varying cultures and practices of the other races. "The Mylare', she said 'spit on the ground to ask, do we share this earth. The other must spit back in accordance to be accepted." The other three voyagers spit in remembrance as well. So with the act of friendship and acceptance in place, they cautiously followed the Mylare man into the settlement he presided over.

The Hufore group looked around and immediately remembered the trees and soil they were taught by the High God. They asked if they could set up lodging during their visit. After getting approval, they swiftly took down limbs and large leaves, gathered grass and shrubs, procured a multitude of vines and rocks and thus created a shelter, large enough to cook inside as well as house all four members comfortably for the upcoming season. The lodging was grand, especially compared to the shabby barely standing tents set up by the local Mylare. When the four Hufore members finished setting their gear inside, they returned to the circle of the encampment. All of the Mylare people were regarding them with wonder. It astonished them that this new race could one, move so quickly it almost seemed like the wind, and two, build such a grand thing in only a few hours. "You said you came to teach us, right dark ones?" asked the chief Mylare. "Then I say yes, teach us to build like you. You will stay until we know your ways, and you ours."

The Hufore group was at first pleased, but then it dawned on them that the trip they expected to take a full season at the max, may in fact take a good deal longer. Nevertheless, such was their destiny as the High God commanded, and follow it they would. They retired for the evening in their brown and green cabin. They wept. For the first time in their lives, they would not be sleeping at their homeland. Yes, they wept.

They were awakened by a voice singing. It was soft and pure, and high like a bird. The gatherers told them of different songs they would sometimes hear, but this didn't sound like any of them.

True and true are the ones who fall, back to the mother tree they go. Life in grace or death disgrace, back to the tree they go.

Dragon's rage and fires burn, all take heed to know. Stay on true, the paths will glow, or back to the tree they go.

Life is good, old Mylare knows, he stayed true, to the dragon's oath. So when breaths last for Mylare old, back to the mother tree, they go.

Then, peaceful and in sudden unison, the Mylare people chanted. *Back to the Mother tree we go*. The sound was so soft it seemed like only one person was singing it, but the four friends were watching them as they were collectively holding hands around a pit of fire and chanting the beautiful phrase. It was then that the four Hufore realized, they were to not only teach the other races, but they were also supposed to learn them as well.

The team spent the next few weeks showing the people of the village various other plants that were of use to everyday eating and living. They took down more trees and branded the wood to use for better buildings and tools. They showed them how to clear out an area, burn the ground, plant crops that will grow and feed for seasons to come. However, while there, tragedy struck. The rapid new growth of the small community attracted the attention of the Dark Mylare, who apparently lived little more than a mile away. One day, while the communal was upgrading another lodgings for its members, a newly trained gatherer and trapper was out collecting the morning rounds when he saw the protruding foot of a felled Mylare man. He ran towards it and moved the shrubs that were blocking the body. Though as he knelt to find what wounds befell this man, he was harshly struck in the head. He fell unconscious... When he awakened, there was a small community of Mylare, standing around a fire. At first glance he assumed he was found by a member of his own village. However, upon looking closer, he realized that their hair was not the simple white and green of his people, but white with different colors. He slightly rustled at the stark realization. Unfortunately, he was quickly heard, and a tall man walked over to his location. Leaning over with a sharp object, the fear the boy felt was confirmed when he saw the piercing green eyes of a Dark Mylare.

The man pulled him across the ground by his hair towards the group and cut his palm. He held the bleeding hand over the fire, as the chief of the village quickly strode over. He grabbed the young pale Mylare by his neck and squeezed it until he began chocking, but right before the boy went limp he released him. Two dark Mylare grabbed the injured man and the chief began questioning him on the intruders. He wanted to know why they were there and how long they would be staying. He asked where they were from and if they were friend or foe. And once he was finished the interrogation of the young Mylare, he smiled and made a gesture to the two men.

They immediately took action and lifted the teenaged pale Mylare over the fire, savagely burning his thin chest and torso. When they were finished the torture they then spread mud over the burning flesh so it would cool. In some instances, men would pass out from the shock of their bodies cooking, but unfortunately for this soul, he endured the scorching pain. It was as unpleasant an experience as the young man or anyone of his village had ever endured. He had heard stories from the neighboring village about the methods of the Dark Mylare. While he lay there writhing and seething in agony, he wished for nothing more than to be back at home, helping his father gather herbs and setting the traps for the small animals. Finally, after three hours of torrid pain, the cool mud finally kicked in, and the young Mylare went into a much needed, deep sleep.

When he came to, he was being carried towards the sounds of water. It was the deep river that branched off from the grander Claupine River. It was how his ancestors found this land to settle. It gave them fresh food and water. He knew it as a source of life, as well as a source of fun on summer afternoons. Now, he was sure, it would be his tomb. However it was not as he thought. It was worse. The Dark Mylare waited down river, until the pale Mylare visited the fishing nets of the water. They were cleaning their gear, tools, and utensils when the Dark Mylare sprang into action. They quickly dragged the struggling teenage body to the edge of the deep stream where they knew after a few minutes of the busy work, they had to check the last trap they had been leaving there since the new people arrived. They cut both of the youth's wrists, and then took his tongue. After that, they cleaned off the dried mud on his belly and chest. Then they placed his arms in the water, laying his body out so that the exposed burn wound would be faced upwards, raw and receiving the unwanted sun's heat. Then they retreated into the forest.

Unable to speak, tongue-less and tired, the young man moaned as loud he could to get the attention of his village-men. But they could not hear him over the sound of the moving water and their conversation. Eventually one trap gatherer wandered down stream to check the last trap when he found the dying body. He screamed for help and the entire party went to observe and help the pale, long bodied teen. They took him out the sunlight and asked what happened, but they quickly realized he could not speak. They hurried the dying young man back to the village as swiftly as they could. The boy's parents came running to see him. They tried to wake him up. He would not stir. It was Norgei, the single female being comforted by a Mylare man, who saw the crimson wrists in all the commotion, still dripping small drops of blood. "It is too late, I fear. His wrists have been severed, and he has lost much blood, too much to be revived. I'm so sorry for your loss my friends."

The young pale Mylare teen, even more void of color due to his lack of blood, opened his eyes one last time when the crowd began to chant, *Back to the Mother Tree*. He reached his hand towards is father, and then pointed at the grand central tree from which most Mylare villages surround and smiled. Then, his hand went limp. His red eyes dimmed and closed.

From the first day awakened to this world, the Mylare developed a special custom. After the head was bitten off by the dragon and the body devoured, they buried the head under the mylare tree that gave them life. Thus in death, the heads of nearly all deceased Mylare are dismembered and buried under a tree, often times of their choosing.

As was the tradition, the leader of the community would honor the family, and release the head from its dead body. As the young man wished, his head was placed under the tree and buried. The winds picked up speed and the Mylare saw it as a sign from the High God. They began their chant again but were broken up by the sound of the dead teen's mother. She began singing a soft song, as she sat, looking over his tortured body. It was a life cut immensely short. For the Mylare are of the trees, and as such, have longer life spans than any of the other races. They can live, with good health, up to two hundred years. Seeing a young one, not past his teen years tortured and murdered was too much sorrow for her to accept.

Watch your step, and be of thee, Dark Mylare will consume your soul.
One, do you, two, with me, Fear the green eyes whole.
They watch from trees, the Tinted skin, and take and take you know.
Keep your wits oh Mylare please, with the Dark ones, heads will roll.

She clutched the body during her hollow tune, shaking with grief. Upon finishing, her mate took the body away. Bugt and Ghortu traveled with him. They returned after sunset and blood stained their light fitting clothes. They wore the bland look of murderous revenge on their faces when they left, and when they returned, it was seemingly the same. Bland and distant they looked, but not for revenge. It was the guise of men who wanted justice, but after receiving it, realized it would not change what caused the original pain to occur.

Nobody of the village asked what happened, for they knew. But Norgie, being of the Hufore race, had the strongest urge to know what happened. That night, she asked her new partner, a Mylare man from the village, to accompany her to the Dark Mylare site in the morning before the sun rose. He asked her not to, but she insisted. Still in a new state of infatuation, he agreed.

In the morning, right before the sun was in the sky, they departed to the site. However, as soon as they reached it, Norgie wished she had not. Throughout the camp were bodies strewn across the ground. They were all dismembered, and not in the headless way as was the custom. The heads were scattered as was the true form, but there were also legs, arms and torsos covering the land. The bodies were opened and mutilated. It was a massacre. The men recalled their vengeance upon the group. But it felt wrong to the Hufore. She actually found herself feeling a bit of sympathy for the people of the accursed village. They suddenly heard the strong sounds of wings beating. She looked up and saw three dragons flying by. The Mylare man reflexively hid inside one of the buildings and beckoned for Norgie to follow. Then unexpectedly, two women and a child came out of a shelter. They each grabbed two of the nearby heads and took them to a tree. While they were doing that, the young child lingered, looking at the bodies once inhabiting her village. She let out a wail and fell to her knees. Suddenly the three dragons swooped down upon the only three survivors of the massacre. They rounded the villagers and roared at them. One stalked off and began eating the body parts. Another roared at the group, snapping at them for intimidation. The third told them to quickly feed on the dead and leave. He devoured many body parts and flew towards the nearby river. The second, and most aggressive of the trio, asked the dark Mylare which of them wanted to be eaten by the hungry dragon. At this, Norgie dashed out toward the group. The dragon, distracted by the sudden extra person lost focus. The Dark Mylare members dashed to the closest enclosure. Seeing them, the hostile green dragon leapt to cut them off. The rust colored dragon looked on, but did not interfere. He simply kept eating the body parts of the dismembered party.

Without thinking, Norgie, fearful of the green and gold dragon, took a sharpened stone from the ground that was once owned by a member of the Dark Mylare and threw it forcefully at the dragon's large eye. It did as she wished and hit the dragon in the eye, causing his rage to soar at the agony. He roared and backed away, trying to appease his hurt right eye. With that small window of opportunity, Norgie, as fast as her air nature could carry her, ran and retrieved the three remaining Dark Mylare members. They were just outside the enclosure when suddenly the green dragon dove on them. All got inside the small enclosure except the eldest women. The green dragon with gold tint held her against the ground with claws dug deep in her sternum. The woman yowled and begged the dragon to release her, but it was too late. The infuriated dragon devoured the lady entirely. Still not satisfied with the old, lean meal, he charged toward the building to devour the bold woman with hair the same color as his companion. He stood tall on all fours, breathed in the air, and let out a blast of wind to destroy the lodgings. As it fell, the Rust dragon with ruby tint leapt in front of the raging dragon. "You had your meal, Tyrge," boomed the satiated rust dragon. "Now leave them alone. Your eye will at least get better with time, though it will never fully heal. That is the price you pay. We were not supposed to eat the living of the species, as Sherygha commanded. Now join us at the flowing water to drink, and then after a few days we shall take our leave." Then he strolled through the forest, rubbing his scales against the hard bark to clean them.

The green dragon growled and hissed at the quartered group. He wanted to kill them all for damaging his eye, but he knew better than go against the larger dragon's dictation. He did, however, spit the oily acid all dragons have on the group, leaving burn marks on their bodies. Then he leapt into the air with an angry roar and departed the ruined site.

As the group entered the encampment of the Pale Mylare, the chief quickly ran to meet them. He saw the Dark Mylare mother and child and spit in front of them. They looked down for a moment, and spit also. With formalities concluded, they were rushed by the populace and an abundance of questions. After giving them herbs for the acid burns, they explained that everyone in the village was awakened by roaring dragons and once they gathered, they immediately realized that Norgie and her acquaintance were missing. The duo told them all that happened, still in fear of the raging wind dragon. They told them how they found the bodies of the people, dismembered and head unburied. They also spoke about seeing the three last members and the ordeal with the dragons. Tired, hungry, and still aching from the acid, the two went to the food pit and grabbed breakfast. Then retreated to the newly improved hut they built together.

Unsure what to do Bugt decided to return home. He told Hufore group his plans, and bade the community farewell. He knew he would be back in a week or so, so he left a few items in the large hut that housed him for several weeks. He left out for his home, alone and worried. They were supposed to simply be a friend of the people, to become one with the community they were to help. He direly wanted to return home, see his queen and friends and be at peace. He traveled the three days and upon returning home, he was immediately saddened.

"Where is the village?" asked Bugt of the Queen Hufore. "Why are so many gone? Has tragedy struck our people?"

"Be at ease," responded the queen. "Like you four, I have sent others to do the same in other lands. There are three separate but larger expeditions underway. I have received locations of various other small villages consisting of the other races that have been springing up from passing dragons. Crude they are living and it will be a disgrace if we do not as we were created for. Please my friend, inform me of the Mylare living in the forest."

Bugt sat in audience of the queen and told her of the tale from the first day to his last. He spared no details and when he was finished, they ate and drank the ale made from the grass roots. Then they slept.

The moon was high and the air was cool when suddenly they were awakened by a loud rumbling. "I require food and drink immediately," rumbled the highest dragon, Rynesch, to her guardians. "My slumber has drained me, and I require nourishment." The dragon stretched long and wide, and then continued, "While some of you gather this, I need you, Bugt, to recite me the entire tale. More importantly, tell me the part about the dragons. How much time has passed since my hibernation?"

The workers sprang into action, getting the largest

pieces of prepared meat and filling the baskets for dragon tending with fresh water. While they moved and prepared the meal, Bugt and Zharda sat adjacent to the dragon and retold her of his tale. Upon mentioning the dragons, the dragon let out a low growl. While Bugt completed the recounting, Rynesch finished the first basket of fish, and glugged the entire bucket of cool water. She thanked Zharda and the Hufore for her care the past three years and then launched herself into the sky. She flew unevenly at first, as her wings had not been extended in over three years; nevertheless her disgust with the green dragon's behavior heaved her to better heights, letting the wind carry her to the destination.

She spotted the three dragons flying only a few miles away from the kill site. She roared and hailed them. All three landed, surprised to see the actual sky queen Rynesch. They were young dragons, only hatched a few years ago, probably at the time of her descent into a coma, and had only heard of the enormous Sky dragon. And now, as she flew above them, she puffed up her size and spread her wings as wide as she could. Looming above them, silver and sapphire, she seemed as vast as the sky itself. She sucked in the air around her, cocked her head and blew out a wind so strong that it blasted all three dragons away for over a mile. As the sky dragon, her wind assault was so powerful that it turned into a massive tornado, destroying the landscape in its wake. After taking the direct hit, all three dragons were injured. So Rynesch dove on the green one with the lamed eye. She hit him directly with the horned crown on her head. Then she sliced open his torso and ran it up through his neck with her nose horn, eating not only his liver, but also his two, still beating hearts. She then, in a rage, tore apart the lame beast. He disrespected not only her creator but also their proctor, by curbing his appetite on the still live flesh of the young species. She then spoke to the other two dragons. "You dare disrespect the order of this world. We are dragons, here to protect and guide this young species, not to instill fear and feast upon them whenever we desire. The High God as left us many animals, both grand and small, as well as the vegetation of the earth, to keep us full and strong. I have heard they have a tantalizing taste, but if I catch any dragon guzzling on them while still living again, I will only offer the same punishment as that green and gold one laying in pieces over there for the buzzards to eat." She landed and directed her attention, "You, dragon the color of rust, I also know that you simply watched while your comrade behaved so dishonorably. For you, punishment will not be swift." Rynesch quickly jumped on the young dragon, bit off its tail and swallowed it. She watched him move in circles, scrambling to find somewhere to relieve himself the Sky Dragon's fury. But alas it was barren land, wiped away by the storm she sent for retribution. The rust and ruby dragon kneeled, and cowered before the massive dragon. She walked over, head raised high, and thundered "Do not cower before me. If you would have followed the rules, told to you in the egg with your clutch siblings, then this situation would not have happened. Yet, the anger over the impudence of my dragons awoke my senses and fetched me out of three years of hibernation and despair. And for that, former drake, I will not kill you. Now go, before I send another storm in your direction, leaving you to spend the rest of your years as a large crippled lizard." Rynesch whipped her tail around, lodging multiple horns in the side of the little dragon. Knowing he would eventually heal she pulled away her tail, and then leaped into the air, found a strong breeze and began searching for her friend and captain, the black and gold dragon, Sherygha.

FIRST AND SECOND DANCE

When the Hufore group of eighteen reached the narrower part of the raging Claupine river, they immediately set up camp. They cleared the land, using all of the resources to their advantage, as was their custom. The rations were in surplus so they created the modest village to house them until they could craft the proper types of boats needed to cross and navigate the striking river. Being at one of the narrowest points of the river, and accessible to endless supplies, another project was to build a great bridge, able to withstand time and a multitude of passengers. It was decided within the group that multiple bridges should be erected at the narrower edges. Many and smaller rivers and streams were formed from this vast river, thus the group would follow lesser waterways to branch out to the other races to impart knowledge in them.

During the two years they lived in the first settlement, seeing dragons was a common occurrence. Often times the creatures would land, converse, help in some way, then feed and sleep. The Hufore group loved when they did, though it did many times make them miss the prodigious Sky Dragon. They learned even more from the visiting dragons. They found out that two dragons will primarily mate with each other for their life. Though, unlike the young species it takes three years for a clutch of dragon eggs to mature; and a year before that to actually be laid. And unbeknownst to the dragons that had their first eggs on the planet, a dragon had to use a power they are given from birth to soften the egg for breaking. If both parents were to die, the egg would stay intact, hearing the outside world through dreams and memories, but never fully awakening. So the dragon race began going off to mountain sides and creating mating caves called clutch so they would remember where the hidden eggs were sited.

They also learned that the properties of the power that they are born with are also what they draw strength from. Earth dragons eat rocks, land and boulders to replenish their power faster. It also strengthens and brightens the scales. Water dragons use water, wind dragons use air, fire dragons use fire or lava, ice dragons deal with ice or the cold air of the atmosphere and the extremely rare lightening dragons follow storms to swallow the lightening. Any food will make a dragon happy, but the elements are needed for shinier and stronger scale coats and giving extra power boosts.

A third thing the people learned was that dragons born of this world will not grow as large as the ones who crossed the arch of the heavens; however the unlimited life span is still equal. Drakes and drakka will mature and grow its wings within an earth's three years; and after that will grow in size for another fifty years. However, being that their origins are of the timeless land, upon reaching the fiftieth year and full size, aging stops and unless killed, will live forever.

It took the travelling Hufore group two years and three months to complete the projects. Upon completing of the bridge, they packed what could be carried, and crossed the bridge, leaving the settlement for the next group of explorers to use on their journey.

However, one single group did not leave the settled land as they arrived. Two separate groups did. It was always an easy decision to build the bridge connecting the land from the river gash, but where one group wanted to boat up the river so they could see the settlements on either side, the second group believed it to be more beneficial to trek through the land, branching out more to affect more people than only the ones who settled on the river. Thus on boats, six people departed, two married and four single. The remaining members, now up to fourteen due to two childbirths, waited three more days to depart. They left instructions for the next inhabitants and began the life long voyage to explore other cultures.

The petite group traveled along the river for two weeks before they saw another civilization. From the distance, the people looked much the same. Assuming that it was somehow the other group they divided from, they approached them. As they neared the small settlement however, they quickly realized it was a different race of people. The trees were not cleared and the housing was primitive at best. Three branches, covered with mud and leaves, and placed against a tree was not any type of lodging a Hufore would use with such abundant resources available. There was rotten food and what looked like tools flung all over the living space. A weak rack, holding only three fish leaned over so much it looked as if it would snap at any moment.

No, this was not in any way a base camp inhabited by their kinsmen.

The group signaled to each other and all directed their boats towards the mediocre founding. As they neared, they could see clearer features of the other race. It seemed weird to look at a group of people, so similar yet so different. Their skin was not smooth. The Hufore were darker brown skin, much like the raw wood they extracted from the forest, while this new people were brown, but lighter, like after the wood has been shaved and treated for usage. It was like comparing a maple tree, deep, dark and rich, to a lighter oak, common and expected. Also the eyes were lighter as well. A brown color compared to the black of the Hufore people. Yet also, the hair was the same but different. Their hair was red, standing out against the green area they lived, but compared to the sunset color of the travelers, it seemed again, plain. They talked amongst themselves before reaching the coastline and agreed it was like seeing the first versions of themselves. They remember hearing about the first group of the species, the Norfex, but when described, they seemed more dissimilar. Yet seeing this rustic race as they closed in to greet them, felt more like meeting distant cousins.

"Hold," screamed a Norfex man by the shore. "Who are you? And of what are those vessels you use?" Suddenly, the rest of the villagers appeared as well. They all ranged from infant to elderly and eager to see the strangers approaching.

"We are Hufore people, and I believe you are Norfex," answered one of the women of the group, Gyl. "We are not here to harm you. We wish to spend a few nights with you as we travel along this river, if you allow entry of course." After a few moments, a larger man, robust in the belly but solid in the arms and legs stepped forward. He smiled and motioned for them to enter what was clearly his establishment.

The group landed, unloaded the gear they travelled with and took the boat out of the water so a high tide would not carry it away at night. They met each of the settlers and were told they could create a tent like the others. However, knowing a better way to sleep, they began the task of building four separate, small tent shelters. They took the same basic thoughts of the Norfex, but instead of using one side for cover and placing against a tree, they made the two sides bigger and sided them against each other. Then, the more intelligent newcomers placed a heavier wood splint into the ground for the tent's stability. They each loaded their respective tents with personal belongings and began making and setting traps for fish and small animals. While the tourists moved with extreme efficiency, the Norfex watched with both amazement and ignorance. It seemed to the Norfex, as if the visitors had done the tasks hundreds of times prior to reaching them. They at times would ask to help or to even learn what was going on, but each time the Hufore would deny the request and exclaimed they would show them once they finished.

At nightfall the group gathered and ate the salty dried meat they brought from their home with a piece of bread as the Norfex set a small fire. The fire contained moist wood and would often come close to dying. They learned that each community of Norfex settlers appointed one or two persons the much needed job of fire keeper. They were to stay up during the night and ensure the flame did not die, as well as keep scout for predators. So the first thing the Hufore did was to gather dry wood and grass in the dark forest. Then, after showing the unknowing Norfex the difference, they created another fire, slightly larger than the previous. It was the first of many occurrences that the Hufore travelers would step in to instruct the people of the village to have a better way of living.

The Hufore, finally able to rest, unpacked their sleep sacs and began a much needed rest. Right before they retired for the evening the village leader asked how long they would be visiting. "We will be here," answered Gyl "for as long as it takes, kind chief." The camps elder looked upon her with a look of puzzlement. She continued to explain, "We are nomads my friend, wanderers like many of your race. Charged by the High God to travel this massive land of Choi, imparting knowledge and wisdom as well as assist our other brethren of the six races to leading better, more productive lives. We, my friend, will try to teach you and your clan all we can do. So we shall not be leaving until the task is done."

At that time, the wise and powerful dragon Sherygha was flying overhead the massive three island cluster named Mageek by the Ormaque inhabitants. He had left the community of empowered people to seek a mate. The old dragon had been around since before the planet was made, fighting in two wars for the High God in the timeless land. He was given the elemental powers of fire and ice to protect the planet and named proctor of the world. Unless killed he would not die, as was the destiny of all dragons, so time seemed a trivial matter. However, as of late, the strongest dragon on the planet began to feel pangs of loneliness. For the past year, he would leave for weeks at a time to seek a mate. He wished for a crest full of horns. She would have to be strong but nonetheless sleek. Yet, most of all, of good character and wise, like him. Once, two years ago he had thought such a dragon existed. She was exiting a small river, scales shining from the water and bright sunshine, when he noticed her. She beat heavily from a full belly towards the sky, then, after catching a breeze, let her body glide to the fresh air above. Sherygha watched as the dragon, another black like himself, but with silver tint easily rode the breeze with freedom and ease. Her outstretched wings were elegant and narrow. He watched, as she extended her long graceful neck, piloting her body through the large open air. Judging from the size of her horns on her spinal ridge, the mesmerized dragon guessed her to not be of eternal age, though not far off. He took to the sky behind her, still fixated on her presence. The dragon, oblivious to the stalking Sherygha, flew northwest.

She whipped the slender, serpentine tail and abruptly changed direction. The female dragon landed right outside of a cave, obviously inhabited by Uckleet recently. There was the usual litter of people scattered around the entrance. As he was landing behind her he could smell the stench of a species not accustomed to regular bathing. Yet, the smell was not as strong as the magnificent dragon he was following.

Upon reaching the ground he sniffed the air, full of a female dragon's musk. He had smelled it for thousands of years, yet somehow, this day, it exhilarated him.

He slowly and proudly walked toward the enormous cave entrance. He breathed in the great aroma. The cold of the mountain felt good against his hot body. Puffing up his chest and lifting his head high, the black dragon looked like a moving scaled boulder. He peered into the cavern and looked around, letting his eyes adjust to the dim light. He took a step inward when suddenly a hard loud blast of fire spread across his broad, muscular face. He looked upon the cave wall as the she dragon was lunging towards him. He assumed she was going to use the nose horn all female dragons are born with to attack him. More enticed than upset, adrenaline pumping through his entire body, the large dragon quickly backed out of the cave, hoping the dragoness would follow. She did indeed follow, thinking Sherygha injured and fleeing from her. Upon reaching the opening, she was immediately on the receiving end of a fire blast this time. She dug her impressive nails into the ground to keep from falling back against the attack. However, when she looked up to respond, the slick elegant dragon was startled. She was taken aback by the enormity of the chasing dragon. Standing on all four massive and muscular legs was Sherygha. He stood broad bodied with his thick scaled neck held high. His head was large and broad, even for a member of their species. His horns were huge, pointed and long. Some even the size of or bigger than the digits on her hind claws. His Black scales, large and shapely were gold around the edges. With his wings extended, they shaded the very sun. She had never before seen such an impressive dragon. He was magnificent to gaze upon, but he would have to earn her respect. The retort he gave her was strong, but she was stronger. So she would have to test his mantle completely to ensure he was a dragon not simply of size but also strength. He would have to be strong enough to defend her while she held and raised his clutch from any and all adversaries. Although, regardless of how he did on his test, the smaller dragon very fetched by the size of this stalking male dragon.

"Tell me, oh lord of the skies," teased the smaller dragon, "how was a dragon of such size able to stalk me for so long before I realized it? The other male dragons who thought to take wing behind me were loud beating brutes; savagely attacking me after the same little fire nudge I gave you. Quiet in flight and still able to think after an attack, you are not the same as the other males that attempted to mate with me. However you will still have to prove yourself, black dragon." Laughing she quickly she took the skies, beating her elegant wings furiously to gain distance from the black male. She caught a strong wind and it propelled her further. Instinctively, Sherygha followed in chase. They were in the first of the mating dance, the flight dance, given by female dragons to test a male's strength and skill in the air. If a male cannot overtake and outfly his potential mate, then she will not give an opportunity to become lifelong mates. So the shiny black dragon maneuvered with the wind. She would lift higher and then dive towards the earth. Before hitting the ground, she would spin and correct herself and fly low, tail horns scraping and tearing the landscape. She would also curve a treetop as if to settle, then launch into the air, do a loop and head in another direction. However, any trick she completed, Sherygha was able to follow. Then, above a small pond, the grand dragon overtook the smaller, knocking her into the water below. She landed hard, but before she could fix herself and make her escape back into the skies the large dragon pinned her down with his front two claws. He only pressed enough to break a scale or two, but it sent her the message he was conveying, ***I am not your equal. I am your superior.*** Then he swiftly turned and struck her harshly with his tail. As she reached landfall, another unexpected blast of fire braised her hind leg. Beaten, injured, and yet enticed, she watched the massive dragon as he took a drink and steadily walked towards her.

"I am not a simple dragon, growing from the knowledge of only this world. I am old and wise, older than this actual world in fact. I was taught by the High God and have become the wisest of our species. By your horn growth, I would say you have not yet reached your fiftieth year, but are very close. Tell me, young dragoness, are you aware of what happens on your fiftieth year." After the fatigued dragon shook her head no, he continued, "Amongst the wisest dragons, we call it the Eternal Year. That is the point where you no longer age, though you will possibly still grow a bit more in size for another year. Most dragons born of this planet are unaware of this, as we do not tell them, but there are many that do. Though, young dragon, you were thinking correctly. I do not think as brutish as other dragons and for that reason I am not sure that I desire you to mate with." Sherygha looked away at the floating clouds, and then added, "I require more than a simple dragoness to spend a possible eternity with. Search the heritage memories you had given to you while growing in your three year shell. Tell me my name and I will consider you for becoming my life mate."

The young black female dragon began stepping

forward. She dipped her head and dug up some of the cold ground with her nose horn. Her eyes swirled, as she lifted her head, recalling the memories left to her from her ancestors. Suddenly, as if struck by lightning, she gazed upon the wise dragon with slight trepidation. "I do apologize, great one. Your name is Sherygha, the proctor of the earth. Bringer of balance and as you said, wisest of all species on earth. I am sorry that I did not realize sooner. I have heard many stories, but never imagined you, of all the dragons on earth would desire me as a life mate. My I ask" nervously the dragoness asked of the black and gold dragon, "if you do not mind, why have you decided to wait so long to choose a mate? Any single dragon would love to accept a mating offer from you and give you many young drakes and drakka."

The large dragon chuckled. Then he assisted with the celestial power that all dragons share and healed her injured wing, arm and hind leg quarter. He used the time to calm himself down from the constant burning feeling of wanting to mate with her. He also used the time to consider his answer. He turned away and looked at the distant mountains they just departed from while in the first mating dance. "In truth, I never had the urge to. Knowing that I would never die from age, I spent my time enjoying the planet and its inhabitants. The final species, like the race of Uckleet that inhabit that cave you lured me to, live short lifespans. Even the Mylare, who can achieve a few hundred years on this earth before their hearts give way are nothing compared to that of dragons. As a result, they breed swiftly. Generations upon generations have been born in this world. They are a lively species, and can do many things when guided in the right direction. So I focused my attentions on doing that, guiding the Ormaques of the enhanced lake into a population of strength, honor and prosperity. Until I noticed you, fair dragoness, taking flight out of the small river you were bathing and eating in. It was the first time in a few millennia that something stirred in me to have a lifelong partner, and foster multiple clutches with. Now that I have answered your questions young dragon, you will answer one for me. Tell me, my beautiful black and silver queen of the sky, what my dear, is your name?"

The dragoness halted, realizing she never thought to offer the greatest male dragon her name. Then the brightest of ideas struck her. He was not a dragon to be impressed or happy to simply boast his power. He would need not only a physical test, but a mental one as well. She decided that instead of a physical dance, she would ask one that tested all his wits. So in the sweetest tone he had ever heard from a dragon, she told him "I was born to my parents on the eastern side of a range of mountains facing the superior lake; up north in the winters' cold. My mother died to the barbarian species of the Arfaet as many dragons have. Giving their children a chance to escape, they took the full attack of the smelly creatures. My father is forever injured, though now I finally understand why he did not die, still sits on our clutch shelf, too high for the Arfaet or the nicer Uckleet's ropes to reach him. They took two legs, a wing and his life mate before he used the rest of his strength to climb the shelf with only his front arms. Leaving him desolate and unable to move, my father feasts on the small cave animals except when I or my siblings stop by to bring him food and fresh water. Take him a large serving food and water for me. After he has eaten, ask him my name. Then dearest dragon, come find me; though I will travel with the wind. When you see me again, tell me not only my name, but also my parents. Then, and only then, will I gladly do the third dance with you, making us mates for life. I trust in your abilities. If all I heard about you are true, then you will come back to me and I shall give you many clutches." Then suddenly the female dragon lightly nipped Sherygha on his tail, a sign of affection for dragons. When he turned to face her, ready to question this new test, she hit him with the strongest blast she could muster to his nose. He jumped back and dipped his head in the cool water. When he did, she hit him with her tail and ripped the leather skin of his wing so he could not follow as he had earlier in the day. Once he lifted his head, he saw that the young female was beating furiously and had gained a distance he could not easily catch in the condition he was in. She turned and yelled back, "Find me soon and tell me my name, great Sherygha."

It took the old dragon a few months to find the exact shelf of her birth. The mountain range was larger than he remembered, and many dragons choose the isolation from the fastest reproducing species to let their eggs mature the 3 years needed. After finding a multitude as egg shelves, Sherygha smelled and followed the hard stink of the brutal Arfaet mixed with the rocky stink of the Uckleet intermingled to a high opening. As she promised, an old, lackluster red dragon, looking almost pink for years of lacking sunlight was laying there on the egg shelf. He was lying with his mouth open, waiting for a large rat to wander onto its tongue. It was a disgraceful way for a dragon to live. So the large dragon walked up, and told the dragon he would take him outside to feel the sun and eat of fresh, hot blooded, prey so long as afterwards, he divulged his name, and the name of his former life mate and female child that is of black scales and silver edges. The maimed dragon first laughed and coughed at the demeaning dragon, then told him to leave. However, Sherygha was not a dragon to be trifled with by any species, including dragon. "I am Sherygha, high proctor of this land. I do not offer idly, and what I offer seems very reasonable. Do as I ask and I shall fulfill my promise." The father of Sherygha's infatuation was about to speak, but coughed again, dry and hard against his ever healing lungs. He looked at the black dragon and nodded in agreement when suddenly the black dragon grabbed him by the wing that was still attached. Weak from years of being fed by others, the father could not attempt to fight back. Sherygha grabbed him by his small dragon body, feeling more like a young drake than a master of the sky, land and sea. He took the dragon off the shelf, spotting a small community of Uckleet and Arfaet staring at the sight as he departed the cave. He reached the outside and kept flying, his massively built wings propelling him toward the slightly warmer climate of the blood thirsty Arfaet race's beginnings.

Once Sherygha found an opening with wild rams, he landed downwind of the grazers and placed the tired dragon against a rock's edge. He thought about telling him to stay still, but did not want to seem insulting. He took to the sky again, unable to quietly move through the small forest due to his girth. He flew overhead again, letting the air carry him higher so he would not have to beat his exhausted wings. Luckily, a larger ram moved away from the group to work down a piece of land. The dragon, ready to eat more than feed, tucked his wings against his back and darted towards the unsuspecting ram. Right before he would have normally stunned the animal with his tail he outstretched his front arms and grabbed it swiftly by its horns. The determined dragon beat his aching wings harshly, to gain altitude and clear the sparse trees. Barely above the treetops, the dragon carried the franticly bleating ram to the dragon that would determine his future.

Right before he reached the immobile red dragon, the left wing of the food bringer gave out, causing him to crash into the trees. He covered the prey, even though it was kicking its hooves trying to find ground. They landed with a loud thump, sending all loose particles in the area scattering across the forest floor. Kicking its hooves and bleating for his life, the ram tried to escape the dragon enclosure one more time. But even bruised, hungry and exhausted, the old dragon was too strong for the little ram. Without opening his eyes he addressed the waiting dragon. "I have spent nearly all my strength, to recall and fly you from that dreary cave shelf and to feed you as a true dragon should. Eat this ram, alive and fresh so you will be pleased.

The old lackluster red dragon slowly dragged himself towards the dragon claiming to be the great Sherygha. As he neared, a plump ram being held by his large curled horns, was trying to back away from the enclosing dragon. Suddenly, without any realization of how, the muscle memory of a dragon fresh on a kill took over. He thrust his open jaws to the neck of the gift, roughly brought to him. He bit through the flesh, feeling the last rapid beats of the animal's dying heart. The warm blood trickled down his scaled jaw and pooled on the ground around him. Once the animal went limp he opened him up, eating the tasty, nutrient rich insides of the sacrificial ram from the bush. Then, like a dragon starved, he began eating the rest of the animal. For minutes he fed, gaining small portions of strength as he had not felt in decades. Immersed in his own hunger and greed, he paid little attention to the exhausted dragon that not only flew him to this outside land against cold northern winds, but then fed him live game, thus renewing some strength he hadn't felt in years. Bits and pieces of the animal went flying in all directions as the red dragon feverishly devoured the large, live kill.

Slowly, and close to comatose, Sherygha croaked, "I have held up my promise. Tell me the names I need. Then the most graceful dragon I have ever seen will be with me forever, and give me many clutches." The red dragon, full for the first time since his daughter visited two years ago, ate some rock that were lying about. In only a few moments his scales regained a bit of color and vitality. His claws got stronger, and he roared. Proud and strong, even if maimed, the red dragon roared at the downed dragon. "You want my help, but I do not care to give you my mate's name, nor my black scaled daughter. You are unable to fight me, tired and powerless. I will consume your large body, then be strong enough to carry myself further south to the warmer climates. As for me, I shall tell you my name. It is Gruibi, stupid dragon. It will be the last you hear, foolish dragon. Why would I tell you my daughter's name, so she shall leave with her own family and forget to take care of me when I need it? No, that will not do. If you were the real Sherygha, I would not be the one with the advantage. So I truly don't care how or if you flaunt his particular colors, just lay there, be quiet and die." After a moment of sinister laughter, Gruibi continued, "actually, I have decided I will tell you. Find my beautiful green and silver clutch mate in the afterlife and tell her I will grow strong again." With that, the dragon softly said the names of his daughter and her murdered mother. He then ate another mouthful of dirt with rocks in it and swallowed, preparing to shoot a blast of earth at the dragon lying before him.

Sherygha, having the vital information needed, gathered the remainder of his strength and climbed to his tired hind legs, extended his massive wings, all while towering over the disabled dragon. Enraged with the cripple dragon for betraying him, he boomed, "How dare you? After I risked my health and strength to assist you, I get treated as if I am your enemy. You, I promise will pay for that treachery. I have her name, and her mother's as well now, but you have forgotten what mine means. So please, fragile dragon, let me remind you of my power before you die. I AM THE GREAT DRAGON SHERYGHA! I was made personally by the High God himself and strongest on this world!" The giant black and gold dragon huffed in the air and roared as loud and broad as he could at the cowering red dragon. Then he blasted the earth dragon's tail with ice, freezing it to the broad connecting joint. Then he stomped down on the tail, shattering it. The Elder dragon then bit off the second wing of the red dragon, while he was still screaming in pain. He then burnt the fresh wound with the power of his fire element. In avid fear for his life, Gruibi began pleading with the second oldest dragon on earth. Alas, it was too late. The dragon was filled with contempt and rage for the disgraceful dragon. He grabbed the Red and took to the sky, his anger dulling the original pain felt in his wings. He scanned and found a small tribe of Arfaet settlers near the ocean. He flew there, unknowing to anything else in the world at the moment. He hovered over the settlement, watching as they grabbed their miniscule arms and rock shields. He went closer and told them this was the dragon from a cave north of them. They cheered and waited as Sherygha dropped the lump of a dragon off to the most brutal of the barbarian races. He landed and told them emphatically that this was the ONLY dragon he would allow them to kill without seeking vengeance. He then took a grazing animal off with him into the distance to eat. After devouring the animal and drinking from a large stream that was fed from the ice of the mountain above, Sherygha slept deeply. Once his body healed, he would return to Mageek to replenish his power, and then search for his life mate, the fire dragon of black and silver, Ellydra.

After a year of searching for her, Sherygha assumed the dragoness fell into despair with the increasingly troublesome Arfaet race. He would leave for weeks looking for her while he patrolled the land, but still to no avail. She stayed in his mind as he did the regular patrols of Choi. Yet, as time continued to pass, his Ellydra seemed farther and farther away. So with sadness, the dragon gave up on finding her. However, the unfortunate dragon had been awakened to the urging of finding a suitable life mate. He did the flight dance and enjoyed it. And to top it off, the cunning little dragon sent him on an adventure to win her heart. Now, the female variety of his species seemed plain, obvious, needy, or wanting.

He descended onto one of three large platforms made for him by the Ormaques. They had grown as a population again, without his realizing it. The High God took parts of various creatures to facilitate the power better in them, but that act seemed to make them have slightly more animalistic qualities than the other races. His Ormaques seemed to only mate during two seasons. Thus, most of age groups were fairly equal. They also move more like schools of fish, or flocks of birds by walking around, following the mass and talking amongst themselves opposed to individuality. The only exception came when it was time to use their power. They each developed in their own way. For some reason, the first thing each Ormaque does when realizing they have power within them is to shape shift. Most transform into what they call mermaids. Some others would change their arms to feathered wings. The older generation would mimic the dragon by changing to a beastly body, take the head of a bird, and grow wings to fly like a griffin. This generation was growing steadily in their abilities. Like dragons, each child of this race was born with a natural affinity for an earthly element, though they could not wield it as easily or in high amounts like the dragons that lord over them.

"I have returned from my patrol. How are things here on Mageek?" asked Sherygha of the students, gathered for his arrival.

"There were a number of dragons stopping by to drink of the lake. One even saw through the barrier of hiding and came looking for a meal. I'm sorry, but we had to hurt her to subdue her. I know you don't want us using our gifts against others, especially dragons, but she was relentless and even attacked one of us while out on a swim"

"Tell me where she is. I will deal with her more severely," responded the slightly interested dragon.

"We created a charm to keep her in the water. Since she is a wind dragon we wanted to keep her away from air," said one young man twirling ice in his hand in attempts to practice his control. "I can show you where." Then the ice swirl got larger. The boy focused on his ice power ball, increasing it until it matched the size of his head. He then lengthened it to an arrow and launched it into part of the lake between the second and third islands, where there was still no habitation.

Sherygha drank large mouthfuls of water to replenish his energy and power, in case it would be needed when confronting the intruding dragon. He flew around the large islands first, checking on the progress of the young species and visually announcing his return. Then he landed on the only ice patch in the middle of the lake. He shifted his eye slits to endure the water and dove in to see who was being held hostage. He did not see the entire dragon, but from the immense size, knew immediately that it was someone he knew from the timeless land.

"Why have you attacked my friends, dragon?" inquired Sherygha. "They would have killed you had I not warned them against doing such. What do you say for reason's sake?"

"They are a strong race," responded the captured dragon, "but they did not beat me like I was some simple minded drake, fresh from the egg. No. I willingly got captured to wait out my time until you arrived in peace and quiet. It really was a nice time playing hostage. But now that you are here I would truly appreciate you releasing me, *Captain* Sherygha."

Immediately he sprang into action dispelling the binds he taught them to quell a dragon. "I apologize, Sky queen. In the water, I could not fully see your color or tint. I am sorry the Ormaques were not more cordial."

"Nonsense. Like I said, they acted exactly as I wished. I knew that there had to be power here. Especially being that this is the empowered water. I saw the barrier and remembered you were directed with herding the Ormaques into fulfillment. Though, to do a sensory dispeller, they must really be thriving under your tutelage." At that moment Sherygha freed her. She mouthed and consumed many from a school of fish swimming by at the wrong time. Then she darted underwater to the island. She climbed atop the quiet island and shook the water off he glistening scales. Her second in command followed, and then opened his wings, letting the water drip out and drying the leathery flesh in the warm afternoon sun.

"I overheard the Ormaques talking about your disappearances the past year. What is the reason; may I ask, for the recent gaps in your advisory?" She continued to prod her old friend, "the people who live here on, Mageek I believe I heard them say, informed me that you have seemed different. Why, my friend, are you changing after such a long time? Is it that you are ready to settle with a mate and after watching this sometimes unsavory species populate the world, have decided to have a clutch of your own?"

Sherygha bristled, startled at the candidness of the highest ranked dragon. They had discussed many things over the millenniums of knowing each other. She only once asked him about his need to sire a clutch.

At the time he laughed and told her that a cave shelf full of drakes and drakka, and a mate for life would stifle his freedom on this new world of paradise. So to suddenly bring it up, while he was just losing hope at that very possibility seemed almost uncanny. "I will not be populating the planet this day. I leave and survey the land. I mark and notice the many settlements springing up across the land." He paused for a moment, then continued, "Although, there was one dragoness I wanted to sire many clutches with. I won the first mating dance of flight, but realizing I was not a normal dragon, she sent me on a quest for the second dance, engaging not only my strength, but my will and wits. Unfortunately, she has seemed to vanish before I could show her I fulfilled the request she asked of me… She was beautiful, Queen Rynesch, beautiful and elegant. Our clutches would have been strong with my strength and stunning with her attractiveness. She was black like me, but with silver edges, a long graceful neck and slim serpentine tail. I have never seen such a well-fitting dragon dame. But she has been lost to me these past two years, and I fear I shall never find her." Then, to change subjects, "Alas, you have not come here to hear me prattle about such matters. How may I be of assistance, your highness?"

"I told you before," responded Rynesch, "I do not need such pleasantries from you. It is absolutely fine to call me Ryn, like you did for years before joining my officers' squad. And, since you asked, I came because there was a dragon that ate a darker Mylare man. His impudence woke me from a three year slumber I seemed to have entered after our creator left us. I erected justice from them and reminded them to warn the young dragons that we, you and I, still lord over this world." She then turned away to depart. Before she left she said, "I wish you luck, handsome dragon, on finding your life partner. One day, I hope to find such a dragon to win the first dance against me, though I am unsure I ever will. The only one that I believe could actually perform such a feat has never wanted to with me." She looked back at the massive Sherygha, bit his tail tenderly, and then took flight. There had only been three times in the large dragon's life that she cried. The first time she cried was during the second war in the timeless land, the second when the High God left this world for the last time, and now. Rynesch loved her second in command since he was a young dragon, wings barely opened on his back He was only a few clutch set younger than her, and always strong, just as the High God intended when making him. She, being the first of all the High God's creations, saw him grow, not only in strength, but also wisdom. She would have given all to be his life partner. As was such, when she was offered any dragon to be her proctor for this world, he was immediately her response. Yet, as time moved, they became friends, close friends, but still only friends. She would try tempting him into a mating flight, but he always took it for playfulness. She even asked him once what he thought about taking a mate, and he had laughed at her. Hurt and embarrassed, she never asked him again. Now, after thousands of years of being next to him, she was finally ready to formally invite him on a mating flight. Only to find out it was not she, which he wished to mate with. Both of Rynesch's hearts ached with sorrow. The only dragon with the ability to best her in the first mating dance of flight and second dance of power, and the sole dragon of her affection since his creation was completely oblivious to the yearning she felt for him.

Rynesch wept as she soared above the clouds. She loosed small roars, angry and saddened. She surveyed the world the High God promised her. She loved it, all of it, and yet, at this very moment despised it. It was not the home for the multiple clutches of eggs she would give Sherygha. She would not spend eternity, rough housing, mating, conversing and showing affection to the strongest and best dragon she knew. There were only a few other dragons from the timeless land that could even attempt to compete with the proctor in size and strength, but none of them had the same intellect and wisdom as Sherygha. The powered blood in Rynesch boiled. She was becoming increasingly agitated. She spotted a small flock of dragons. They all bore fresh wings, and each left leg bore a red stripe, probably a family trait. She deduced they were all siblings of the same clutch and migrating or were training the new wings. They landed in an open field and began the rough playing of dragons. Then, a copper one with emerald tint looked up at the sky queen, focused his eyes with malice and youthful play at the same time. He then breathed in a large amount of air. He launched himself into the air and once he got close enough to the hovering dragon, let loose a blast of wind. Already pained emotionally, both hearts beating rapidly and seething with frustration, the miniscule attack by the young ignorant dragon was the last straw for the Sky Queen.

"This is not the day to bother a sizable dragon such as myself," roared the infuriated dragon. "I am often referred to as Sky Queen. Yet, of all dragons, I do not yield simple wind like you weak dragons born of this world. It is more accurate to say the elemental power given to me is a STORM! And with this storm I will destroy your entire clutch for your audacity" The emotional dragon sucked large amounts of the high air, roared the loudest she had ever in her lifetime and released a torrential storm.

It was a storm that devastated the land. It initially knocked all four clutch siblings into rocks, knocking them unconscious and severely maiming them, probably for life. The trees in the area were uprooted tossed from the land. A nearby village she never identified was destroyed. Bodies were flying around lifeless with the herd of animals they once tended. A gaping hole, once filled with water, left the evidence of the sudden destruction of the land.

The storm ravaged the land, moving in whatever direction it desired for three days. It eventually reached the vast ocean, and picked up strength as it waded outward to the indefinite water. Rynesch left the cave she took shelter in and surveyed the damage she caused to the landscape. However, there was nothing thing there but bodies of desert. The storm, strong and malicious in nature, picked up everything, including some of the Earth's surface, and delivered it to the ocean it retreated to. There were no dragons lasting the beating. There were no people around. There were no villages. There were no trees, ponds, rivers, lakes, or hills and mountains. It was as if the High God wiped the earth again in the storm. The weary dragon flew off towards the northern most mountains of Choi. She needed to grieve her losses. And knowing that the ice dragons were generally the largest of her species, she would have a better chance to find a mate in that area. Rynesch decided that she had two hearts, and though Sherygha may hold one, the sky queen resolved that she could spare the other and still have a good life. That is, if another dragon could actually pass the first two dances of flight and power. She flew harshly. It seemed the storm she provoked even took most of the air in the area. She glanced back at the desolate landscape. It was a scene of pure annihilation. There was nothing left, except shattered earth, anguish and despair.

ELLYDRA THE BLACK

When the second Hufore group departed the village they erected for building, they decided to walk alongside the river, opposed to canoeing upward against the south flowing waterway. Though they walked for weeks, the group was not tired. Composed from the air element, the High God built the race for a highly nomadic lifestyle. Along the journey, a black dragon flew by and landed by the river's edge not far from them, black with silver edges. They could not tell the gender at first, since the dragon was drinking the fresh water, but she grabbed a good size striped fish and lifted it out of the water. Seeing the nose horn, the group relaxed, knowing that female dragons were more sociable and less aggressive than the males. A twig snapped while they crept towards the guest. She quickly turned, intrigued by the sounds of whispering. Attuning her ears to the wooded area she realized it was a group of the final species. Knowing better than to harm one, she turned to leave. However, before taking flight, one threw a sharp rock, loosening a scale in the process. She turned to the group, anger swelling, but before she could decide her reaction, an older man spoke up. "We do not mean to offend. We simply miss the presence of dragons and would enjoy your company and wisdom. In exchange, we can make a camp for few days and tend to your feeding and cleaning. Will you indulge us, beautiful lord of the sky, earth and water?"

Flattery was a dragons' only weakness. They knew it when they heard it, but softly purred anytime they felt it was genuine, even if they didn't want to. She gently laughed and settled in her place, allowing the group to achieve her position.

"Dear mortal, you do not need to flatter to keep me around. Nor did YOU," the black dragon hissed, addressing the thrower, "need to attack me to get my attention. You simply had to ask, and I would have heard. Now create a pallet for me to rest and bring some food, since you are inviting yourself on my meal time. Ask me what you wish to know while you produce, my new friends."

The group was moving throughout the forest, searching all the trees and plants that could be used to their advantage. Rocks would be beneficial as well, but most loose ones are swept away with the fast moving river. Some gathered materials while others prepared traps for the evening meal and breakfast later. They all knew their tasks and worked diligently to finish them. "What is your name and element?" asked a younger member of the cluster, tying three pieces of wood together as a part of the animal trap. "Where are you from?"

"I am originally from the northern caves. After my parents were killed by Arfaet barbarians, my siblings all scattered. I came south for the warm climate and multitude of dragons. My element is fire. And my name is Ellydra, daughter of Gruibi and Allagira."

As the pleasantries subsided, they brought two medium sized fish for her to eat while another of better size was fetched out of the river. She swallowed the fish whole, then ate the second, and then quickly drank the large hollowed rock they used to store water. She then continued "I have been searching for a black dragon like myself, but more powerful. I sent him on a fool's errand, but when I decided I would tell him and save him the embarrassment, he was nowhere to be found. I have been searching for the past year, but still have not found him. I dare not ask other dragons, for saying his name invokes fear, and instead of telling me, they send me in a random direction for fear of his coming to see them. Now I am lost. Not in a directional sense, but internally. I was being coy with the great dragon, and it may have cost me one I want as a life partner." The black and silver dragon looked towards the sky, deep in thought.

Suddenly there was a loud crash as a large tree fell. The dragon abruptly stood, looking towards the sound. Slowly a group comprised of three races, Uckleet, Dark Mylare, and Arfaet walked towards the dragon and the now stilled camp. They bore crude versions of swords made from dragon claws, and daggers from the teeth. Dragon scales of pale red were roughly made into a type of armor for the stout Uckleet and broad Arfaet. Boiling with anger at the sight of the almost pink scales, the dragon loosed her fire bladder in the green forest. The party scattered in various directions, trying to avoid the dragon's wrath. She dashed from the ledge towards the armored people. Knocking over smaller trees and spitting more fire, she was ready to attack the smelly species. A tall Mylare jumped behind a tree and threw a rock, trying to gain the attention of the dragon. When she turned, two of the Arfaet men attacked the dragon, cutting through the thinner scales on her arms with the weapons created from dragon parts. She jumped back and roared at the group, fury rising in remembrance of the childhood assault on her egg cave and knowing with whom the scales belonged. The group tried to flank her from various sides. Seeing the entrapment tactic, Ellydra decided to take to the air. She began spitting at them in hopes of the burning acid slowing their progression while she tried to take advantage from the sky. She first grabbed a larger tree, scaling it to gain some altitude when an assault of crude wooden spears barraged her wings. Three went through her leathery wing flaps, denying her escape. The Mylare, taller than the other races, slashed at her long tail. She shrieked at the damage and released her fire bladder. She sent it farther and hotter than she ever had before. The forest, already covered with her oily spit in all directions, became an inferno for the assailants. Ellydra jumped into the blaze, attacking the mortals, one at a time. Her claws and jaws broke through the thin vines holding the scale armor. Her fury and fire blinding her, she did not see the little Uckleet man jump on her back from a tree. He landed between two horns on her spine ridge, and stabbed her in the side. She bucked and twisted and rolled to get the little man off. He eventually was impaled through the torso by one of her horns when she hit the ground, but he continually pierced her hide until she ended his life. Her back was free, but she bore holes and deep gashes around her spinal ridge and neck. Too wounded to keep attacking, she was backing away. Directly behind her was the river. There were only three left, and even though burned, they still bore the armor made by the dragon scale of her father and the smaller daggers made by his teeth. Her heartache was too much to bear at the moment and she knew there was limited time before they would reach and overtake her as well. Thinking on the battle, it was the youngest species' best tactic. They were not all that strong, and none were as smart as the dragons, though the Hufore seemed compatible, but they could rally together and outnumber dragons easily. Sometimes they could outnumber by dozens to one. A dragon could defeat a multitude given the circumstances, but even a strong dragon had their limits.

Her tail was dipped into the water, cooling the bloody sliced wounds. She needed time to heal. She surveyed the site. Many bodies lay about; the forest by the river's edge was rapidly burning. The light natured Hufore were on the other side of her, hiding in the trees opposite the fire. They were smart and cunning, but not strongly built and could not help her in the situation. She then faced the three nearing assailants. She breathed in the smoke near her, building her elemental power. If she were to die, it would not be an easy death for them to achieve. She roared one last time towards the triad. They halted, not scared but inquisitive. Her roar was meant to be a menacing, blood thirsty roar of a strong, hungry dragon, but instead was short and weak, and what's worse, they knew it. Being a small distance away, they began charging towards her. She had no choice, she would have to fall into to water and let it travel her in its flowing direction if she wanted to live.

Yet, suddenly the three stopped cold, their eyes staring in horror above her. They began shaking and looking for a place to retreat. She could smell the sweat of the species, and even urine from one. Then a massive roar that quaked the earth, thundered above her. Abruptly a massive black dragon with gold edges landed between her and the assaulters. His tail curled upward in accordance of trying not to harm the injured black and silver dragon. "Ellydra, back into the river and cool your injured body. Stay below the water's edge and I will bring justice to you," demanded Sherygha. He then nudged her along with his tail. Once she was covered by the river, he jumped into the sky. He noticed the Arfaet man taking the lead, and figured him for the leader. He dropped on the man, pinning him into the ground. Then he lashed out with his tail and whipped the second Arfaet into a swiftly burning tree. The third, a stout, round bellied Uckleet, was quickly retreating. Sherygha blew his ice breath and froze the little man in place, then crushed him under the massive weight of his front claws. He backed off the nearly dead Arfaet and spoke to him, "I know that your race has been hunting dragons. I see the armor and weapons you bare are from my brethren. I was asked to sometimes stay out of your species affairs, but I am also the peace keeper of the planet. Today, you attacked a dragon, very special to me. For that I will show you no mercy." He looked at the Hufore coming out of the trees and watched them fetch Ellydra out of the river. Seeing her badly injured and in need much recuperation, he yelled to the intelligent race of the species, as well as the man before him "Dragons are not for hunting. We are lords over this world, but companions to all who ask. Tell all as you migrate and do not force my fury on this. For if your species decides to continue on this path, I shall destroy you along with this planet." Sherygha then leaned to the ground and breathed a soft heat instead of a full flame. He would not burn the Arfaet warrior enough to kill, but he would leave him scarred and grotesque for the remainder of his life. "Do not show him any quarter or mercy," he directed the Hufore group. Then he launched to the river, grabbed his future life mate and ascended directly for the land of Mageek, where she would heal and be with him, forever.

****

As dusk began to fall, Hikothe decided it would be better for them to set up a tent and camp for the night before it got too dark. He began unpacking the tent he was carrying while Hikune was getting a fire ready to warm the meat and bread they packed for the night. It was a beautiful sunset, with hues of red, blue, orange, rust, silver and black. “It looks like all the colors of the dragons, doesn’t it grandfather?” asked the boy with awe. Hikothe watched with pleasure as his grandson’s understandings of the world were completely changing. He grew up tending dragons. He talked to them as pets and loved them like family, but now he was finally beginning to understand them as beings. Much like the old man had so many years ago when his father showed him the book and told him the contents. Though, Hikothe was a teenager at the riding age of sixteen when he was opened to the family secret and truth of the world. It was the age he opened to truth to his son, Hikarge as well. However, his son could not handle the vastly different knowledge. It drove him crazy, consumed with trying to deal with the new reality. He mounted his dragon one day, with no destination in mind. It was the last time anyone from Aimone heard from the once prince. The great feeling that filled the Dama could not be explained. He feared Hikune would reject the history like his father, but instead he embraced it, was now slowly implementing it into his everyday life, and still desired to learn more.

"Hikune, this is knowledge, known only to our family. We only pass it down to the future Dama of Aimone. Even your cousins do not know this great wisdom. I was unsettled giving you this knowledge this early. It has driven many insane also, unable to cope with the new understanding. Because of this, I was going to wait. Yet, you were so interested and fervent in learning the truth once you found the book. It is as you said, learning its contents will not only make you a better dragon rider and future Dama, but by knowing the history and nature of both dragon and man, it will make you the very best at both." Hikothe continued, "Once we reach my dragon, he will also be able to use his ancestor memory to assist in the tale. You will have the knowledge only a handful of people on this earth know, but it will be your charge to use it wisely. It will also be your charge to keep it a secret, until you heir a son of your own."

The two sat down, listening to the nature surrounding them. They ate in silence for most of the meal, and then Hikune asked something that had been on his mind for the better part of the day. "You say that only Sherygha is black with gold tint and edges correct, because he was made by the High God?" After his grandfather nodded in agreement he furthered the question, "then what will happen if my dragon is hatched, black and gold like the egg holding it? How is that possible?"

Hikothe finished a spiced drink of ale and settled the canister back into his pouch. Then he addressed the youth's inquiry. "As you know, a dragon's egg will show the colors they will bear in various ways. Always a base color, the color of the primary scales, then stripes, swirls, speckles, or dots will indicate to us the secondary color. As you also know, dragons, like humans, take the traits from their parents, though dragons more so than we. Yet dragons can also take a recessive trait from their grandparents as well. The egg you tend, like the one your father did, holds a direct descendant of the powerful dragon, Sherygha. It is quite special my boy, special indeed. Only a few have been born with the powerful Black scale and gold tints. My dragon's mother was a black with silver dragon, like her own mother. Remember, a dragon will learn while still in their egg, though they cannot be hatched unless helped by another of its kind. So I believe that the egg you protect is the son, daughter, or grandchild of Sherygha. However, before we get into that, I suppose starting from the beginning would be better. As it would be, explaining this part is exactly where I left off. Settle yourself for the night, and I shall continue the tale until you sleep. Hikothe took his ale back out and drank a few more mouthfuls, thinking about what kind of future his grandson would have as a rider. He tucked it away and let himself drift off to sleep, again, as he did most nights, thinking about his lost son.

SUMMON SHAMAN

"**Sherygha settled after flying a** few hours. His wings were tired from carrying the second dragon. It was a few dozen miles before the forest hiding his lake approached, and another day of flying, maybe two from the extra weight. The dragon had too many responsibilities to ignore. So he blasted the earth creating a trench. He placed the injured dragon inside. He landed on the earth above her and breathed his celestial power over her to aid in her healing a bit more. Though, as he already knew, it would not be enough, but he had to help when he could. Still unconscious, he formed slight dome of ice above the dragon, and covered it with the dirt again. It looked like a slight mole hill from a stranger's perspective, so he first retreated back to blazing forest. He reached it in half an hour without the extra weight. Still engulfing the woods the dragon first sucked in as much water as he could. He spit it out over the scorched land, hoping to quell any embers that may decide to reignite. He then flew straight upwards towards the frosty stratosphere. The ice wind and air served just as the dragon wished. He breathed in the icy air to enlarge his entire body, and then dropped towards the forest. When he reached the still havocking flames he loosed his ice breath. He turned his head left and right, making sure to fully subdue the massive burn. He had to exercise complete control. He was the strongest dragon on the planet, and if he got too excited or carried away, his frost could freeze half the landscape. He also needed to conserve energy as he had to return to his mate.

Sherygha put out the fires and left the trees around it snowed in. He created a frozen desert, but the rapidly moving fire would no longer destroy the wooded area and the settlements they housed. From his height, he noticed more villages than he first thought to be in the area. The species were indeed, repopulating faster than most of the others. It also seemed to the dragon, that they were finally, after thousands of years, gaining knowledge.

He flew back to the injured Ellydra. He shattered the ice dome to find her still sleeping. He figured as much would happen. When deeply upset or wounded, a dragon can go into a mental cocoon for periods of time. The hibernation would allow the mind to settle around the recent events and the physical wounds to heal. He sealed the chasm in the earth again, and then flew in direct flight to the lake of the Ormaques. Upon arrival he noticed a few things flying around. It was the Ormaque people practicing their abilities again. He landed on the first and most populated island and beseeched for someone to summon the healer of the land. When he showed up, Sherygha spoke, “Shaman, I need your assistance, immediately. Gather pouches of the lake water and follow me.” He then drank large amounts of the lake water, replenishing his power and verve.

He flew to the outer island, the one he decided to keep for himself until the quickly growing species used the first two and needed the space. He kept a heard of various green eating animals to feed on when in the area. He devoured a smaller one then grabbed a fatted hog when Shaman arrived. The medicine man and healer, Shaman, transformed into a mermaid and began swimming. The dragon, still holding the now stunned hog, took to the sky. He beat his massive wings, gaining high amounts of altitude. He looked back to make sure the healer could keep up when he startled. The Ormaque, Shaman, sprang out of the enchanted water, pouches in hand and with a glimmer, grew legs with claws, a long scaled torso, wings for arms and a flexible tail; essentially changing to a young dragon. Shaman, saying it was the closest a person could get to transforming into a dragon, called it a wyvern. It did indeed look like a young dragon from a certain view. Though, a young dragon under three years would not have wings. Shaman, one of the strongest of the Ormaques had been practicing his changes for years. He achieved the closest to dragon he could with this form. So Sherygha and Shaman flew towards Ellydra. The old dragon wondered how the new wyvern form could keep up his strength over the miles, but assumed that would be a discussion for another day.

As the Black dragon reached the site, he noticed a large hole in its side. He closed his wings against his back and darted nose first towards land. He abruptly straightened out his wings to capture a small portion of air and landed. He peered inside. There was nothing. The black dragoness was gone. He looked around in a panic. He wondered where she could have gone, leaving no traces while severely injured. The wyvern landed and changed back into normal form. He said an incantation and clapped his hands. Suddenly the ice cave illuminated. With that they duo could see where she in fact did leave, but climbed the ice and broke out from the top. Sherygha leapt into the air for a better view. He saw the limp dragoness, very slowly dragging her body and then jumping to gain space. She was heading towards another forest. He roared at the escaping dragon. She bristled and looked back at the quickly approaching black dragon, elated. Then, as Sherygha landed, she saw a small dragon-like creature closing in behind him. She, still bruised and tired could not run, but used the last of her power basis to discharge her fire bladder at whom she thought was another intruder. However before the fire could pass by, Sherygha cooled the flame, protecting his Ormaque friend.

"He is with me. It is not a dragon, but a wyvern. The closest form to dragons one of their species can obtain. His name is Shaman. I asked him here to help me heal you and bring you back to our home. You beseeched me with a task that required not only strength, but wits. Well I have passed your exam, and wish to spend eternity talking to you, mating with you, and loving you. Here, I have brought a fat boar for you to feast on. Enjoy it and get better." The doting black dragon broke off the lower part of the male pig's leg for the Ormaque to eat, and then tossed the still live animal to Ellydra. She grabbed the hog, still hesitant. Then she broke off its tusks to keep from gathering any more injuries and bit through its rough skin. While she ate the boar, Shaman, and Sherygha began healing the dragon, overflowing their power onto her. They used the much needed time to heal while she ate. Once she finished, feeling vastly better she stood. The medicine man stood under her wing, using his healing properties to patch the large holes in her wings. When he finished, the dragon was still sore, but would live. She outstretched her wings and knew she could again fly.

"You do too much to spoil me my lord. I sent you on a fool's errand, in a playful flirt. I thought you would never learn my name, since my father was more than likely dead. Yet somehow, on the very day I do battle with men wielding my father's scales as armor, you save me, knowing all that I asked. You are truly a magnificent dragon, above all others."

Sherygha looked away, deciding what his answer would me. Would he tell of all that happened, and his receiving her father's treachery and fate, or let her wonder on his well-being? He decided he would do neither, and both. While Shaman was eating the piece of hog meat, he began his answer, "I met your father. I gave him food. He told me all of your names. Gruibi and Allagira were your parents. He was wasting away. I told him I would return for him. He felt strong enough to leave on his own merit after getting the large meal, however, after years motionless, his body failed him. He fell as I was leaving. He died on impact. I went back and grabbed most of him, as the Arfaet and Uckleet who reside there had already began hacking at him, as you saw. Then I made a blanket of travelling ice to lay him upon, and sent his charring body out to the water. He will burn until the rains douse his fiery tomb." He saw both Shaman and Ellydra looking puzzled, so he answered the silent question. "As the high God empowered me with two opposite elements, fire and ice, they keep balance with the world. So by his creation, my fire does not melt my ice, nor does my ice quell my flame. They can work, side by side, for as long as I live. That is yet another reason why I am the strongest." The dragon, showing his power together created a ball of fire and ice, spinning together, still destructive, and yet, not effecting the other. He then bit off a large chuck of the ball and ate it. The rest he sent into the atmosphere, and most likely the space.

"I'm glad you were able to see him off," responded Ellydra. "He was never the same after he was maimed. I go up there every few months to bring him fresh game, but even then, the visit is short. Now, tell me dear dragon and friend, Shaman, where is it I am to be living now?"

He walked closer to his beautiful dragon. She would be his. Give him not only children, but a life of great conversations, playfulness and mating. He rubbed under her soft neck, the most sensitive spot for a dragon, and then turned. As he lifted she lightly bit his tail in response. Following in the rear was Shaman, back in wyvern form.

Upon reaching the lake of Mageek, he warmed. It had been his home now for a few centuries, and finally, it would be shared with another dragon. Shaman loving water more than anything else said his goodbyes to the couple and while in a diving motion rotated into a mermaid again. As he hit the water, a grey tail and fin followed through. He came up and waved again to the dragons.

"I have been to this lake numerous times to gather strength. I have never seen the islands in the center. How is that so?" asked the smaller black dragon. "I have been looking for you and never knew you were here, hiding from me in plain sight."

"It is a long standing charm I taught the Ormaques to protect them when dragons came to drink and eat of the enchanted lake. It makes them invisible to all who look unless they know the spell release. You will know it too my dearest. And to clarify, I was not hiding from you; I was out looking for you, as I promised."

The two landed on the third island, furthest from the humans. It was then that Ellydra outstretched her wings behind her, lightly toughing Sherygha. She proclaimed, "From this day until death I am yours, great dragon. Let us mate and make a clutch, strong and wise like their father. Come and do the third dance with me." She took to the sky, beating harder than should be needed, but he knew she was not yet completely healed. She then sang a song he had heard a very long time ago in the most beautiful voice he ever heard. He followed her through the third dance, listening to his new life partner while they mated for the first time.

Where are you brave and true? Master of Land, Sea and Sky
Come in the air to meet me drake, when your wings allow you to fly.
What colors shall our clutch be? What colors are true to you?
For I am here, your dragon queen; I'm forever here with you.
Come forth my dragon, champion of dances three.
Come with me, my dragon king. Come to air and dance with me.

RETRIEVING A KING

Hikothe heard the soft sleep of his grandson. He looked upwards at the stars as he lay still in the night. He smiled, pleased that his heir and future Dama of his cloister was receiving his destiny better than he would have ever imagined. The old man saddened, remembering how it had changed his son. Over the years Hikarge became violent, and withdrawn. When his son married and had his first son, Hikothe assumed he would finally settle and process the changes to his view of the world. Nevertheless, still blood thirsty, angry and confused, Hikarge would still take his dragon and attack other villages. Eventually he ventured too far, and came upon another cloister of dragon riders. After one particular battle, with his victory still fresh, a spy poisoned his dragon during the celebration. Not yet reaching his eternal year, the poison quickly spread through the large black dragon. He slowly flew home, taking frequent stops. When he arrived he tried healing his dragon. He tried to end what was sure to be a long slow death for the large beast. He took two vials of blood to create a remedy, but running to the healer he fell and a vial of the tainted blood spilled over his face. He went mad. As was the Arfaet custom of blood drinking, he put the second vial to his lips and gulped it whole. In a crazed rampage, he went into his room and killed his wife. Then he walked down the hall and slaughtered his oldest son, and daughter. He could not find Hikune, for he was out tending his dragon egg. So first he set his manor ablaze, then he mounted his ailing dragon and left. The memory of his son going insane with confusion at seeing the world with a new perception brought a tear to Hikothe's eyes as he wept himself to sleep.

An extensive roar brought the pair back to reality from the nights slumber. They jumped up, grabbing their weapons in one swift motion. Hikothe knew the strong roar of his dragon Hikarge. He began running when he saw the large dragon suddenly land in front of him. A flash of lightening blasted from the immense dragon and struck the tree in front of Hikarge, cutting of easy entry for the humans. The dragon spoke sternly "I do not ask much old man, but I told you to not bother me while I mate with my partner. Why are you and Hikune here? It had better be a splendid reason or I will not be pleasant to deal with."

Hikothe laughed a loud hearty laugh at the dragon's display in front of his grandson. "Back off eternal dragon," he responded. "We both know that you are taking a break after the mating flight two days ago. And if you had not seen us while flying about, you would not have known we were coming. We were not due to reach you until nightfall anyway."

Hikune looked with new eyes at the banter between the two best friends, one his grandfather, the other his grandfather's dragon. He imagined Sherygha, talking in such a manner with the Ormaques, or Rynesch with the Hufore. It was not a relationship of master and servant. Yet, it was not a relationship of equals either. It was two friends, helping and learning from each other. Then suddenly, as fast as the power of his grandfather's dragon, he looked back in awe, remembering that lightning was his element. It was the rarest of all the elements given to the dragons.

Seeing the boy staring at him, Hikarge decided he would display his might again for his oldest friend's grandson. He breathed in heavily, stood on his hind legs and opened his large claws wide. He spit lightning into the morning air while fully extending the giant wings. It was big and boisterous, and he loved doing it for children. He then spoke to the child. "It is nice to see you again, Hikune. You have grown much since I saw you last. You must grow as fast as a dragon. I also hear you have found a black and gold egg, the same colors as my grandfather. That dragon may very well be a brother of my mother. As far as my memories know, there have only been three dragons with black scales and gold edges. The first was my grandsire Sherygha, and then his son, first of all his clutches, died during the houman war. My mother, Ryghari, was black and silver like her mother and mated with a blue dragon. I received my father's blue scales, and my grandsire's gold edging. I tell you this so you know how important it is to take care of that egg, young Hikune. With those colors, I would bet scale and claw that it is my uncle or aunt, one of Sherygha and Ellydra's offspring that survived all this time." The large dragon nudged Hikothe with his tail. Seeing the boy fully understand the names of his grandparents, he knew the conversation that was being held on the way to see him. He added, more to Hikothe, "I see there has been a lot of discussion along this journey. Meet me at my cave with my mate tomorrow morning. Use this time to finish your tale, and see what the future has in store. Then, as I said, visit me in the morning."

The large dark blue dragon outstretched his wings and blasted a bolt of lightning into the sky one more time, then lifted himself off the ground and headed back to his clutch cave.

"Well that was quite the memorable morning I would say," remarked Hikothe. He then went into his sac, drank some water, and pulled out some meat bread and cheese for both to eat while they packed up the camp.

Finished with the morning chores of a traveler, they began walking again, while Hikothe continued his saga. "So not long after the mating dance, Ellydra informed Sherygha that she could feel the eggs forming inside of her. She would hold the eggs for only one year before laying them to hatch three years after. He went to the north of his private island, where there was a small mountain. The land was solid. He could break through it alternating between his ice and fire, but the process was too slow. He could use more force, but it would not only break the mountain, but due to his massive power, could destroy it completely. Thus, he had another idea. He would import a large family of Uckleet members to create a grand clutch cave and egg shelf. The race was great at pulling the rock out of mountains at record speeds, with the right incentive. The dragon would feed them and their families. Also, they could also keep anything they excavated, so long as he approved.

He made a wall of ice and fire behind the already existing barrier of invisibility to protect his still tender and healing mate. Then he flew north, to the original mountains of the Uckleet, where the king lived. He would bargain directly with him to ensure he had the best. After two days flight, he reached the elaborately gated homeland of the Uckleet. Though there were many entrances and exits of the mountain, when showing respect and requesting a civil audience with the king, Sherygha would have to follow protocol. So upon landing, a group of the smallest race of the species began to gather. They were not unaccustomed to dragons coming by, but generally they were only wanting food or wanting trouble. He was asked his reason for stopping by. Sherygha walked to the door and spoke to the watchman. "I am the proctor Sherygha. I am here to see the king of the Uckleet to speak a business matter. It would be a great honor if he would allow me passage to his home, or if he could come out to meet me. As it has been a long flight, I will leave to feed while he deliberates, though when I return I would like my answer."

The dragon turned slowly, sure not to mistakenly hit one of the smaller people. Though strong and stout, they were also quick tempered and ready to battle. He flew away and fed as he promised. Then, the dragon rested in the sun; allowing the rays to warm his scales and body. He slept for an hour then returned to the massive doors, built from the rocks they were created through. He asked his verdict and did not hear what he expected. "The king wishes you to leave," answered the watchman. "He stressed that he has no desire to negotiate with dragons again. We understand this is not a happy response, but for taking your time and coming, we offer you this sheep, already cleaned of skin, to feast upon as you travel home." Then the man closed the body sized slit.

Angered, the dragon roared. He boomed into the doorway, "I am the strongest of all dragons. I have come here cordially and asked an audience. If you will not meet me, I will come to you." The massive black dragon then let loose a blast of fire and ice that made the door quickly shatter. He looked around at the scattering little people. All were heading in the same direction except one. He grabbed him and spoke stoically. "I am sure you have heard of me. If you do not assist me, I shall eat you, and your family. Then freeze your friends and small them with my tail. I will follow you to the king. If you veer off the path, then I will follow through with the threats I have already foretold. Do you understand me, little Uckleet man?" After swift and aggressive nods Sherygha continued, "Good. I do not wish to harm any, but I shall not be treated like a silly lizard. Now lead the way, tiny mortal."

The Uckleet man quickly led him down the large corridors that were built large enough to allow dragons passage. The king was known for consulting with dragons over the time of his life, like that of his father, and his father's father. It was also known among dragons, that the king never went too deep into the cave. The old palace was dug from the ground centuries ago, and it was prime location to stay deep, yet secretly allow escape if anything should befall the caverns such as a flood, earthquake, or mass attack. Thus the walk was not a long one. In fact, it only took as long as it did because even running, the little creature could cover little ground at one time.

When they reached the door the king, a large rounded boulder was in place. The dragon grabbed it and after leveraging himself with his tail, pushed it back into its normal resting spot. There was a multitude of the elite personal guards, many wielding dragon parts for weapons and armor. Fury raising quickly, the dragon spit flames into the large space. He looked around at the running people and saw one hallway, still closed with three, heavily armored men guarding it. He hopped into the air, breathing fire and ice down upon the group. He landed on the ledge, freezing a guardian before just before his arrival. The second was grabbed and thrown across the cavern, slamming into the wall head first. The third swiped at the dragon but was knocked down and send tumbling down the stone walkway by the horned tail. Sherygha hammered open the door, reached in and grabbed the king as he was plastered against the wall with nowhere else to go. He then whipped his tail at the oncoming members of the kings' personal militia. He knocked them back, but took a knick or to on his tail in the process. He jumped from ledge to ledge, freezing and burning anybody that tried to attack or stop him. Once he reached the opening of his arrival, he pressed his belly against the ground, grabbed the little king with his tail, made his body as straight as he could horizontally, and dashed out like a scaled arrow. He did not stop until he was out of the wreckage that was once the home warrens of the head Uckleet governing body and oldest, richest families.

The king snapped at the dragon once they stopped. "Oh my, oh my. Dragon, that was not a very smart thing you have done this day. I will fulfill my revenge on you for destroying the richest homes of the Uckleet. How dare you attack me in my own home?"

"I asked politely. You did not desire to come. So I came and got you. You say how dare I attack you in your own home, yet your species continually attack dragons in their homes and use the claws and teeth for blades and scales for armor. Weapons and armor I am well aware that are forged with your people's tools. I am an old dragon, much older than you. In fact, to put you in perspective, I am older than even this world. I saw its creation and am now protector over it. How dare YOU, little creature, deny MY request, is the real question. You are lucky I am wise and not as rash as my scaled brothers. They would not have stopped until all inside the caved city were dead." Sherygha roared at the Uckleet king, who had suddenly pissed himself. He then regained his composure and continued, "Now, as I stated before, I have business to discuss. So King Dwarfe, I hope you will not make this an unpleasant trip, more so than you already have." Sherygha inhospitably dropped the king, as a reminder of how much more powerful he was than the little Uckleet man. He told the king his plans and offer. The king thought for a moment then agreed to the terms, while adding a few of his own. They returned to the underground palace. The dragon, per his agreement, did what he could to restore some sensibility to the structure. He put out the few fires that still raged, and brought back two animals, a male and female, so they could reproduce in the closed quarters of the Uckleet. A large family of the kings choosing then followed the dragon. On foot, it would take a few weeks, but since time was of the upmost importance, the massive dragon decided he would carry the four males and two females it bursts, though he did not tell them. After walking for a couple of hours, the dragon grabbed the waistband of the oldest and strongest man in his jaws gently, and then with all four claws grabbed members of the party. Lastly, he grabbed the smallest female with his tail and took to the sky. He knew it would be a tiring flight. It was two days at the leisurely pace he took to get there. If he pushed, he could, after eating, do it in half the time. So after setting them down a score of miles later, he told them not to move and created a large dome, encasing the group until he returned. When he did indeed return, the group found a cooked goat for their afternoon meal. While they sat and ate, the dragon told them of the life they would have over the next five or six months. He also found out that the group was not a family, but inmates of the imperial Uckleet court, and if he approved of their work, they would be released upon finishing the project. As the feeding ended, the group picked up their belongings once more. Sherygha told them there would not be multiple stops like before. This time, he would carry them all the way to his home.

He ate what was left of the goat, grabbed the lesser sized mortals, and headed for home. For a while he went directly there, but then, knowing the possible treachery of their species, began to do loops and turns in various directions so the Uckleet members would not recognize the way there. He also entered through the back of the lake, so the Ormaques would not see his arrival. However, when he arrived and passed through the border, he saw three or four wyvern creatures flying about. They did not say anything to the dragon, but they definitely saw him and his Uckleet packages.

He slowly released the members, keeping his wing beats steady and even. "As promised to King Dwarfe, upon the completion of my caverns, I will allow you to go anywhere you want, with the findings you receive from the mountain." Knowing their jobs and happy to be on land again, they followed him to where he wanted the entrance to the cave to be for his first clutch and life mate. They began their six month job immediately. It would not be an easy task to complete. The dragon wanted the entrance high to keep others from entering, and then full of false alleys and holes so again, the young species would not be able to attack his clutch. He then wanted an egg shelf high into the cave as well as multiple exits like the Uckleet king had at his home cave. With the high demand and little time, they would have to work as hard as they possibly could. As they saw earlier in the day, upsetting the colossal dragon would not be in their best interest.

At that same time, the queen Hufore was talking to her many children. She, her children, their fathers and elderly members were the only Hufore left at the home village. She sent all out to migrate and mingle with the other races. It was their job to teach the uncivilized races how to create and utilize better tools. Through that, they would grow as a species.

"Mother, must we go over this again," complained the oldest child. "We know those plants and rocks and berries. I rather learn more about the races."

The queen laughed. Her precocious children always made her happy when she got lonely. She, knowing her duty as told to her directly from the High God, ordered all persons to leave to base camp. They were not to be a people of stability. Built from the wind, they also had to move. Yet, all things have a beginning, and so, after discussing it with the elders of the race, she decided that she and a few of her children would always live at the point of where they began, so all could have a place to return. However, seeing all leave in the different directions, Zharda was sad. Only her lovers and young children remained and many of them would leave too, until they found a mate, and returned to also add to the home village. It was her life. Hard and unfair. But she knew that it must be done to progress the world into reaching its peaks, though she did not fully know why. The high God and the dragon, Rynesch had explained so much to her that first day. He told her so many things, and she, in return, taught all she met. Yet, so many things seemed unanswered and unexplained. Either way, she had to do as was told, or the races of her species would all eventually die off for lack of learning.

One day, a group of tall, men and women approached her at her village. They had blonde hair with olive skin. The men were broad shouldered, with large arms and hands. The women, in vast contrast, were busty, and shapely. They had small hands, necks and waists, but like the Hufore, wide hips. As they got closer, she could see grey eyes. She then knew what she had already assumed; these people were the wandering and conquering Arfaet.

Full of joy at the prospect of having company, the queen met them at the border of the village. She began, "it is a pleasure to have you company in my village. I live here with my husbands and children. I am Zharda, queen of the Hufore race, created by the High God himself." She looked around at how unclean they were, even for travelers. The Arfaet were warriors first and civilized second. They were the least intelligent of the races and Zharda decided she would be the one who steered them towards a better life. "Please, my friends, come tell me your tale while you eat and rest your bodies." She grabbed the closest man's hand to usher him inside, but he swiftly pulled back. Knowing they were a blood thirsty race, she decided she would not fight them, but use her wits and guide them along. She raised her hands to show she meant no harm, then pulled out a piece of bread she had in her pouch of intertwined leaves and vines. She ate a piece, then broke off the other half and offered the other to her visitors.

He saw her break bread and looked at her for a moment more. Then he gestured to his companions and they began walking towards the lightly gated village. He answered with a bow. "Queen Zharda, I am Pluvach, and in my travel I heard word of you. I look for meet with you and talk and eat and rest. Is this okay with you I beg?" After she smiled in acknowledgement he stood and continued, "I am Pluvach, prince to the Arfaet king. I come look for you to help us." They all walked inside the border and sat at the line of large rocks in front of a fire pit.

Zharda beckoned for her children to each bring one dish to feed to the guests. They ate for an hour and talked about general commonalities between the two people. There were very few. Then Pluvach grew stern, he looked at the queen and began, "I need help from you. I hear you the smartest of the races. I see that you people are nomads, travelling and showing the other races things I never heard of. I see your village, more than anything I know. You talk more easy. You clean and healthy. Make us smart like you. Then show us how to kill dragon and eat the meat better."

The queen saw sincerity in his and his people eyes. How could they only want knowledge so they would be able to kill dragons? It seemed incomprehensible. "Kill dragons? No, that is not the way. You need to find other counc…" She was cut off by the large man jumping to his feet and pulling out a large weapon made from the horn of a dragon. He jumped towards her and screamed, "We have come to learn to fight dragons better. You will teach us or I will kill you and your husbands. Show us now!"

Startled and frightened, Zharda jumped to her feet to back away. She knew she had to think quickly or Pluvach would kill the entire village. "NO! No need to be hasty. I said that killing dragons was not the way. The best way to live is to learn how to CONTROL a dragon. Then they will fight for you. It will not be easy though. However, if you stay with me for a few months, the Hufore will show you how to make a dragon your slave and ally. Once they are controlled by you, you will be able to do anything you want with them. So I will teach you how to talk, walk, wash, cook, find food and everything else we can do, so dragons will trust you and then you can learn their ways to governor them." It was a long shot, but they were not a bright race, and if she did not say what they wanted to hear they would have killed her. Dragons could not be controlled or tamed, but that was something they would have to find out for themselves.

They spent the rest of the night talking and learning about each other. Zharda noticed the four dots on everybody's arms. They explained that all Arfaet are marked the second day of birth. Like the dragon did them at the time of creation to show them how to be strong, they take the four sharpest teeth of a dead dragon and puncture the arms of the infants. Some die, but the ones that live become strong warriors and wives. Thus, every living arfaet member has four puncture holes on one of their arms to symbolize strength from birth.

The Arfaet spent the next few weeks learning how to wash, hunt, trap, talk, and build. They laughed at many things for the weeks of work and learning. It often times took three or four times to fully teach them the new skills, due to their low learning ability. Yet, they did in fact, learn. She told them the lessons would end the next evening and she enjoyed their company. At this, Pluvach grew angry. “You have not taught us how to capture dragons Zharda! We have learned, but you have not finished this bargain!”

“But I have, my friend,” Zharda hastily answered. “It is with these new traits that will cause the dragons to befriend and trust you. Then you can learn how to control them. Just wait and see how w…” Her answer was cut off again. This time, the blade was inside her chest. It pierced through it swiftly, just like a dragon claw. She was stunned. After weeks of teaching the Arfaet, seemingly becoming friends, they still took her life without trying to solve the problem. A wolf’s howl was near, but having his own battle to contend with. The barbarian prince looked in the distance to see how far the animals were, withdrew his blade and departed.

She slumped down into the grass, blood pouring from her wound in the middle of her village. She watched as the small wooden box they carried when they first arrived opened and crude dragon armor was pulled out and put on by the men. Then they ran across the village, killing all of her husbands and servants. The four lovers she took and the loyal workers had stayed by her side when all the other members voyaged into the great land of Choi. She had made a grave error. She only wanted to help the people. She thought that if she educated the prince of the Arfaet people, he would share the knowledge to his people and the trend would take hold. Alas, though now educated, they were still no more than blood thirsty barbarians.

The Arfaet group, after killing the queen and men of the village, took all the rations, animals, and seeds. As they moved about the village they heard growls and yelp of two large animals still battling and decided it would be better to leave swiftly before the winner directed its attention on the group. The Hufore hurriedly gathered the children, bundled them together and then burned the entire village. Pluvach, now with a better sense of direction, decided they would head home to report to his father. They had what they wanted, and would teach it to everybody. They spoke better, learned better ways to make weapons and traps, and could identify plants to make better herbs and remedies to heal his people. More importantly they learned the way to deal with a dragon was not to simply kill it, but capture it, and if possible, control it.

WE ARE THE ORMAQUES

Queen Zharda was dead, and her children captured by her killers. The Hufore race was now completely nomadic. They were now forced to completely roam the land of Choi, with no home land to return to. They did not have roots, or a head governing body, so as it would be, each individual group of travelers would stick to, or create their own hierarchy. For the next two and a half years the Arfaet, the Hufore and the Norfex travelled around Choi more than ever in its history. Each had its own mission. The Norfex, being the oldest race of the species were told to breed and help populate. The Arfaet believed they were supposed to migrate also, but to either conquer or destroy. And the Hufore were charged with spreading higher knowledge and learning to uplift the races. The three crossed paths at various junctures along their journeys. Each of the races moved along to the Mylare of the forest and the Uckleet of the mountains. They would often time stay for weeks during a visit, and then move on to the next. However, sometimes a member or two would stay with the group they visited, yet in the opposite, sometimes someone from the stable Mylare and Uckleet would leave with the caravan.

As it was, the races began to become mixed more and more each year. Many settlements were popping up, housing many members of the varying races. Often times, there were settlements or villages, comprised of a race or small mix of races. Many children were being born composed of varying traits, passed down from their parents. Boys with light brown hair had red eyes, and girls with olive skin had long flowing black hair and green eyes. More than anything, kids with white fleshy skin, blue eyes and blonde hair were seen as the Uckleet and Arfaet had been mixing for the longest period of time.

The villages would create a circle with their borders, then meet and mingle at the enclosed space called a market. It was where the races traded their crafts, goods and services. They met many of the other races. Eventually, people would even settle in the market area, to be closer to their product and services. It was the beginning of a multi-national barter system. Each race traded with the other, except the Ormaques. It was as if they were ghosts. Each of the races heard of the sixth race from dragons, but none had seen them in person.

So as the next couple of years went by, these settlements took on the term village markets. Then one day, closer to the second year, a large cabin of wood and mud based at the edge of a lake met a group of other travelers. The various caravans began to settle in separate areas as was the custom. They, as always allowed room for a dragon to land around them. Then over the next few months other settlers eventually came and added to the created village market. Then one day, with the early morning dawning not quite high, the early risers saw a full village appear with the sun. As it was full of mystery, the light rose from the ground to the sky, showing a wholly functioning village being revealed as if from a cloak. An alarm ran through the connecting villages. A mass appeared in the market corner to see the village that literally unveiled itself in just one morning.

Suddenly, there was splashing coming from a group of people that were swimming. They were grey with black hair and had eyes the color of berries. The people looked like the same species, but were yet different. As the people slowly migrated towards the water's edge, the Ormaques went to meet them. They wore light clothes but little else. There were about twenty of them, male and female. The crowd was astonished at the feat of building this large of a village in one night, with such a little amount of people.

A male walked over and began talking to the crowd. "We are the Ormaques, travelling from the land of Mageek. We have traveled here and watched your actions, and have now decided we would greet you and mingle amongst you of the other races." Observing the crowd, he continued "I am Shaman, the healer and leader of this village. Mageek has been our home for almost two centuries. But I have led a group of my friends here and set up a site to be amongst your village market." The group then walked out of their village and toward the populace and began mingling and meeting the other races. It was a cold dreary day, but seemed brighter than any day before. It was the first time, since the creation of the planet that all six of the races were near each other.

For the next seven years they all met and traded and learned about each other. As others came, the villages grew. It became the largest village market of the planet. It grew rapidly. One day, during a meeting with the six heads of the villages it was decided they were to name themselves. Each person had a name for their own race, but there was not one for the entire species like the others on the planet. So the Hufore head, one of the original members created by the High God and first husband to Queen Zharda, decided that he would create the name with the letters of each race so all were to be included. First the idea was rejected and each person offered their own names. Yet, with everyone being biased, they decided to allow hearing the Hufore's proposition. He stood and said, "As I was already here, and noted the order in which you all entered our Chief's Tent. Hufore, Ormaque, Uckleet. Then Mylare, Arfaet, and Norfex. That way, there is no order preference. H.O.U.M.A.N will be the name of our entire species on this planet. As members of our people mingle and mate, creating families, clans and villages for themselves we shall become a fusion of races, as the High God wanted. Your traits will be mixed with mine. We shall all share one body and land and heart. Our different knowledge's will be common. Our children shall be of various backgrounds. We shall not be solely one of six races taking part of a species, but one singe race. Today, we shall tell the world through our travels and others that visit this cloister that we are the Houman race, created by the High God himself to prosper on this planet. Are we all in agreement?" It was a roar of agreement. The speech moved all the village leaders. They renamed the village market. Seeing how the market itself became a living village of its own, mixed with persons like any other and the central nerve of the combined area, they named it Zhivy, the first cloister of the world.

As it was, history has written in many books that the houman race was created at Zhivy. Being partially true, it spread quickly. Each of the village leaders sent word back to their respective kings and queens of the races and told them of the new changes. The name sounded strong, and with hearing it was what the High God wanted, all would accept. So it became, on the seventh year of the founding of the cloister now called Zhivy, the youngest species on the planet forever became known as houmans.

It was cause for a celebration. Shaman decided that he would show the other houmans how to eat a steamed shellfish they loved on Mageek. Shaman and the other Ormaques had shown little in the seven years that Zhivy grew with them there. They would not lie, but not offer many facts about the race either. As Sherygha had warned them, the other races were not very bright or trustworthy. Many they met seemed quite decent, but others, particularly the Arfaet and Uckleet, were liars, greedy, and treacherous. Thus, Shaman instructed his people to not reveal the power they had, or the path to get home to Mageek. He gave them a location, to a small plot of land wiped clean near the ocean, opposite their enchanted lake. Now with the new agreement in place and seeing for himself how the eldest Hufore behaved, he asked him to help retrieve the shelled creatures from the water with him for the banquet.

As they walked, the pale Ormaque was quiet. When they reached his village, Shaman finally spoke, and very quickly, as to not allow any others to eavesdrop. "I am a healer as I said before, but I am much more. We Ormaques are not like the other races. The High God gave us gifts, based on the properties of the earth, like the dragons. At the water's edge I will show you, and solely you, Prince Glaridth of the Hufore. Like all the races, we had a dragon guide, but ours was the noble Sherygha. He warned us of the customs of the other races, but told us the Hufore were the most intelligent created and learned from the High God directly. I see only goodness in you, and because of that, I will only show and allow you, to hold this secret. Will you be our only aid Zhivy? I fear we will need someone wise enough to count an ally as we grow with the other races. I brought only a few with me, yet I already see many children growing with the brown skin and purple eyes. Or they even have grey skin with broad body attributes and blond hair. We have seen them birthed from our race, as well as from other races. I guess such a thing was destined to happen. But it will be soon that the Ormaque genes take hold. In fact, on their tenth year of birth they will change. Watch me, Glaridth. Watch me with your own eyes."

Shaman, reaching the water waved for the Hufore to join him. He smiled, did a shiver, and with a glimmer, his legs turned into a long grey fish tail as he entered the water. He swam around, and then resurfaced. He spoke again to the staring man, "This is the power of the Ormaques. When we reach the tenth year of life, we change onto a half animal creature." He turned his body into a griffin and flew out of the water and landed next to the still amazed Glaridth. He turned back onto houman form and waited a response, and then with a smile he turned into a wyvern and launched himself into the air again. He left the man standing in place as he flew over the cloister twice and then back. When he landed he happily spoke to the Hufore, "I have not allowed changing in the public view. You see, we Ormaques were first made, and on our creation day, turned into the first creature I showed you, the mermaid. All of the animals we come from, minus the ants, need water to survive, as do we. This is why we do not travel long distances." He shook Glaridth's hand and proceeded, "I am the oldest and strongest of my people. The last was called a wyvern. It looked very similar to a dragon, for alas I tried to mimic them for years. But that form was the closest I am able to achieve. Though, in the air I look almost the same. It felt very good to be able to fly in the sun again. I also have the elemental power we are born with, like the dragon race. Remember me telling you?" Shaman then reached his hands forward towards the lake and turned his palms up. Then he clapped them ahead of him and lifted them from his knees to his head. As he was lifting his arms, the water began to rise to higher waves. He then reached to it and seemingly pulled a sliver of the water out of the mass and was swirling it around his body. He then turned the water to the Hufore Elder and smoothly swirled it around his body as well, creating a figure eight binding them. After a moment, and to make sure nobody walks up and sees the spectacle, he took the water back and turned it into a ball, spinning rapidly. Then he launched the ball of spinning water into a nearby plant, knocking it completely out of the ground.

Glaridth spoke quietly, "I see why you kept this from us. I, and the other Hufore, already knew you were made of mystical properties, but this is nothing like what we had thought capable. Your race truly is above the others. I can also see why you fear the youth's born of another's race and your own. It was the High God's will, but I believe it should happen slowly. I will be your ally and protector of the Ormaques' secret. Now, let us take a step back to reality, and for the first full celebration of the newly named Zhivy, show us the steamed shell fish your people eat."

Shaman walked to the edge of the water and again raised his hands, though this time, he turned his palms in a circular motion while doing so, as if pulling the water again. "Get the basket I brought ready to hold them." Suddenly large crabs and shrimp reached the land, enough to full not only this basket, but hundreds more. He grabbed the biggest ones he could, but it would not be enough to feed the hundreds now living in Zhivy. Then, without notice, he swept the remaining creatures into a hole he created with the blast of water. The mud was being driven out by the water, making the hole deeper. With all the creatures inside, it seemed like a small pond. Then, startling to even Shaman, the hole was covered with earth and grass until it looked like a small hill. Both men turned and saw another grey Ormaque man standing there, with an unabashed smile. He spoke to both men, "Hello prince Glaridth. I see our leader has entrusted you with our clandestinely true nature. I also trust that you will not abuse our power or confidence, or we shall return to Mageek and inform Sherygha of your disloyalty."

Glaridth answered the man warmly but firmly, "I am of the Hufore. We spoke to the High God directly. I already knew of your wonderful gifts. I was aware of how you got them, as well as how you can use them. Though I must admit, the shape-shift was more remarkable than I could have ever imagined. Do not fret my friend, I, as well as the Hufore, are allies to the Ormaque people. Now, seeing as how you made the earth move, I can assume you made these clay bowls, though much easier and better made than my people could have prepared. Please make more, enough for us to carry them back to the day's festivity of founding taking place in two weeks." With a nod from Shaman, he did as he was told. They called other people of races to come help carry the loads back to the ongoing jubilee, for there had to be much preparation these next two weeks to celebrate the first day of the now, sole Houman Race.

THE FIRST CLUTCH

"**Wow, that was how we** got the name human, sorry, I mean houman? It seems so weird grandfather, all my life I called us humans, never knowing why. But what happened to Sherygha? Did he leave after he had his clutch?"

Dama Hikothe, still walking, took out a piece of fruit to eat. He bit into the pear, and began, "well to answer your question I will have to retreat back a good bit of years, picking up with the powerful dragon almost where I left off. The time frame of this part runs and overlaps into the same time as the last. Now let me think. OH yes, the last time I spoke of him, he had just dropped off the six Uckleet workers to excavate the mountain and create a private cavern, clutch cave and egg shelf for his future children. They began working immediately.

"The mountain was not high, but very steep; too much for a houman to do by their will alone. So they began at the bottom, and decided to work their way upwards and outwards. They worked hard, as was the prominent characteristic of their race. The workers moved rocks and debris with absolute efficiency. They did not complain often. Ellydra, growing large in the belly and breast with her first clutch of eggs supervised most days. Talking to the group, and even assisting when she could, it was a nice job. Sherygha stopped by at least once a day to check on his mate and the progress of the project. There were many gems that were quarried during the long six months. Unless of gold or silver or black onyx, they were allowed to keep them, though every so often the black and gold dragon would keep a red, yellow, or blue gem to hoard.

One day, during the second month of work, Sherygha was walking to the cave when he heard the noises he knew all too well coming from houmans. He stalked closer and saw one of the Ormaque woman and an Uckleet male mating, right outside of the cave while the others were deep inside having a lunch break. Unsure what to do he charged at the duo as they finished. The man hid behind a tree while the woman, changed into part snake, part beast and slithered off. The people of Mageek were not to be encroaching on this island of the cluster. It was his island until he offered the space to them. This upset the dragon more than the actual act. Houmans mated. Just like any other species on the planet. However, Sherygha warned the Ormaque people about the other races. And to fraternize with them, on his personal land, was intolerable. He would not punish the Uckleet. The first reason was he did not know the rules. Secondly, if he killed him or sent him away, the six month production would be extended, and even though the eggs would not lay for another seven months, it was not something he would chance. So the man could stay. He spoke to the man, "I know your species is more vicarious about mating habits, but if you do, get to it after work my little friend. And I would stay away from the grey Ormaques. They are not the same as you. Now scurry back inside, finish your meal, and get back to work." He then used his sense of smell to follow the fleeing female. He floated above to trees to where she was crying, surrounded by a group of her peers. They all looked up at the hovering dragon, fright in their eyes. He swirled around, deciding what to do. He breathed a cool air, letting the light rain turn to snow, even though in the early part of summer months. The Ormaques wore little clothing to allow swift shifting. The sudden cold was his warning to the people below. He dropped to the ground, hitting it heavily. Then spoke harshly, "I cannot forbid who you mate with, but remember I warned you to be weary of other races. As far as my island goes, the next time you enter without my permission, I will grab you and take you to the farthest place I know. You will not intrude on my space again." He took to the sky and let the snow fall for another hour. Then after a meal with his mate, he breathed fire into the atmosphere, warming the air again.

Still not settled from the event from days before, the dragon spent another night stirring. "Be soothed my champion," Ellydra softly whispered to her mate. "It was a moment of passion between the two mortals. We both know they are a precocious species. Allow the little man and mystical woman some fun. They are only here for three more months or so. Then they can do whatever it is they want. You have promised them freedom. What if they fall deeply in love for each other as we have and he decides to stay here with her, or she, leave with him? Do not ruin their emotion. It will only make you the enemy on both their behalves. As far as coming on the island, they already do it when you are away. That's why the bridge is always in working condition.

Be logical my dearest, and leave them be. Come, rest closer to me and I will sing to you. I believe you work too hard to be losing your rest." He nudged closer to the smaller dragon, resting his broad neck under hers and interlocking their tails. She then sang a slow, soft song to him, one he never heard before. At peace, the dragon drifted to sleep.

The next few weeks passed as they could. He noticed that the Uckleet had made the first exit of the cave, near the end of the island. He dually noted that at the very edge of the second island was the new base camp for the workers. It seemed all six members of his mountain crew had fancied the company of the mystical Ormaques. Sherygha decided that it would be as it were. So long as they continued to work with diligence, he would allow them their evenings for entertainment. He wondered if the Uckleet people knew of the properties of the Ormaque, but deduced that after three months of seeing mermaids, werewolves, wyverns griffin and whatever else they turned into to roam the forest and sky, they little mountain workers had to have realized the truth. Yet, he was concerned. So that night after they worked through a brutally hot summer day, the dragon met them at their new camp with his mate. They landed and the six came out of their enclosures. There were only five structures for housing, and as he thought, one pair came out of one house. They were all mid dressed. Not wearing the dirty clothes from work, nor fully into their fresh evening casual wear either. He brought his tail around, and at the end of it was a bull, large, black, and full of meat. Not the stringy meat of the mice and squirrels that lived on the island, or the little meat of the few fouls and fish they caught, but thick, filling meat that would put a person to sleep after eating it. He spoke kindly to them, "Today was a hot day my friends. This evening is hot as well. You worked hard did not complain. I find myself at fault for putting you in such conditions without also being a dragon of honor. So tonight, we shall eat this bull and talk. Not about plans for the cave, unless they come up of course, but about us. You and the grey Ormaques, and we dragons. This planet as a whole. I will answer any questions you have and we will be friends. Do not invite anyone over this evening. It is one for only us. I am ashamed I have waited this long to have such an evening, but as I stated earlier, that is my rudeness. I have faith you will forgive me." When all had nodded he lightly laughed and continued, "wonderful, my friends. Let me offer you my personal flame for the evening as we cook the meat. And in the spirit of friendliness, let me cool off the air a bit for us to sit comfortably." Sherygha breathed an easy fire into the cooking pit, and then blew his ice breath into the sky, bringing down the temperature a few degrees. Getting extremely comfortable with the pleasantries and new weather, the Uckleet ran inside to finish dressing then returned for the evening.

"Do any of you know how you were made when the High God created you?" started the large dragon. "He took the Uckleet rock, the same one surrounding the palace of King Dwarfe, and molded it right there, in that very mountain. In fact, the same exact spot that the Kings bedchamber is located is in actuality the birthplace of your race. Your people were the second race to be created. I see you looking at me in disbelief.

But I know the truth. I was created by the High God himself thousands of years ago, in a timeless land. I saw him create the world, and watched from a distance when he created each race. It was not until he created the Ormaques, was I charged with a closer role. I was to not only watch them, but also teach them, as the other dragons were supposed to do for their respective races. Unfortunately that was not the case. Entering this world gave us elemental power on top of the celestial, but it also gave us free will. Thus, some of my brethren decided to do what they wanted, instead of what they were told.

"So I took the new race under my care. They are very different from the other five races, as I'm sure you have come to notice." With this, Sherygha looked around the site at the Uckleet. They were all looking straight ahead, as if frozen. They were scared to answer and lie, but knew they were sworn to secrecy from the new friends. Ellydra spoke up, "It is okay, little friends. We know that you already have knowledge of the special abilities of the Ormaques. Do not fret, we are not upset." With that being said, the six persons heaved a sigh of relief. It was as if a mountain like the ones they excavate was removed from their shoulders and they were free again. They looked from Ellydra to Sherygha. He was sight to behold. His vibrant black scales, shining gold and red from this tint and edges against the fire, was like seeing a reflection of a red sun, setting against the black sky. The peaks of his horns were sharp like blades, another defense he held over the other creatures of this planet. His face was broad and wide, much like the rest of his body, but his eyes, most strikingly were gold and green color.

He watched them, and realizing they were all staring at him, he then stood tall on all four legs, his tail held high. Then he extended his wings and let out a strong solid roar. He, as most dragons did, enjoyed displaying their strength for the other species. In reaction, Ellydra, black like him but silver and shining I an almost bronze in the fire light, did the same. She was a small dragon compared to the goliath of Sherygha. It was like seeing the largest mountain in the world rising above the first peak of many. And yet, she was still a force to be feared. She had a strength in her that was clearly visible. As the onlookers watched with awe, they thought the two seemed perfect for each other. They roared to the sky together, eventually ending in unison. It was a moment never before seen by the group, possibly the world, and they enjoyed every moment of it. Then one of the girls began an upbeat song that reminded her of the two dragons.

For there was I, and you noticed a love and lover's true.
So come with me oh fancy thee how time will tell me too
If you are here and I not beware then how fun can we do,
So come together fair and fair and time allow us through.

Then the man she was courting with took up the second verse, going at an even faster tempo. His words were shorter also, made into a quick staccato.

Somebody bring me a rock or three. Three is truly company.
How can you dive for the trees to see, when the ground is beneath your feet to flee
And everything spins like rocks will do
So come together fair and fair and time allow us through.

The third verse was sung in an even faster tempo than the previous two in a merry unison.

Oh how can you tell a rock from stone

When you travel down the hill no longer alone
And looking at each other as lovers do
So come together fair and fair and time allow us through.

When the song ended the group laughed with heartiness that the dragons had not seen in anyone for a long time. It in return, caused them to laugh as well. They spent the rest of the evening enjoying each other's company. Sharing stories and asking questions. The Uckleet admitted that they never thought enjoying an evening with dragons was ever possible. They asked the dragon Sherygha if they could continue to live on the island with the Ormaques. They could make a living as they do now, creating tunnels under the islands and trading what they pulled out the earth. The large dragon knew that they would not be treated the same if they returned to the mountains of the Uckleet. He also did not care to leave his cave often or for long periods of time. Also, if the six stayed at the island, he would not need worry about them telling the truth of the Mageek lands. So he nodded, as was the species' custom. He told them they could stay, be one of the Ormaques, so long as they observed the rules of the islands he set forth. His eldest Ormaque had taken a group to see the world and settled by a small lake. Maybe change would be coming faster than the dragon perceived. They ate and talked until all were full. The houmans went into their houses, and the dragons just slept as they were. Tomorrow, they would go back to boss and worker, but tonight, they would stay with their six new friends.

As time progressed, the cave began taking shape. He helped the workers when he could. Sometimes he heated the rock, creating a small flow of lava. Other times, he froze an impeding rock or mud slide. There were various ways in and out of the cave for the dragons, and even more, smaller tunnels for the Uckleet and Ormaque. The egg shelf, highest point of the clutch cave, was twice the length of the Sherygha from nose to tail, as he requested. No person could scale that height except a few wyverns, but there were three tunnels shown from the ground, and only one went to the actual shelf. There were small tunnels put in for water flow and even smaller for ventilation. There was a room for his dragon hoard and as a surprise, a small bath, deep in the ground, nearing the lava below for him and his mate to soothe themselves.

When the cave was completed, there was still a week left before she released the eggs for their three year development. He told them to retreat to the first island with the Ormaques and stay there while he inspected the cave. He then destroyed the only bridge that connected his island to the other two.

He entered the cave with the swollen Ellydra. He remembered all the niceties they afforded themselves while building. He knew human treachery, and would not allow them, or the changing Ormaques to encumber on his eggs or life mate. Once the cave was completed, he would allow them to settle on the land, with his permission. He went to the vast entrance and blew a hard cold wind. Capable of destroying earth, this feat was easy. He listened and marked where the human tunnels were placed. He went to the entrances and filled it with dirt. Then he burnt the dirt to turn to stone. Once, in the stoned state, he froze it. Sherygha repeated this to all the openings except the first and main one used by the workers. He then went to the cave wall leading up to the egg shelf and released his flames across in a pattern. He smoothed most of the rocks edge, so the little people could not grip it with their fingers. If anyone desired to reach his sleeping children, they would have to use their wings. The next day he grabbed a boulder, taken out in the early days of the excavation and lodged it in front of his dragon hoard of precious jewels and gems. There was also a large supply of the newly craved metals, gold and silver. He took smaller rocks and lodged them into three of the seven dragon escapes. He used the process of freezing a rock to the wall. Then another, and another, until it creates a cone of rock and ice, then sets it ablaze to create a smooth wall. By making it a sharp cone, and then melting it together, it also became a weapon to those who decide to enter from the other openings. He would take no chances. He then set other jewels and luxury items solely for dragon inside the living quarters to offer his mate the most a dragon could want. They then moved into the cavern, their new, dragon motivated home.

Thus, after a year of being with eggs, Ellydra awoke with a stir. She scrambled to the opening for the egg shelf and launched herself into the air. She flew upwards and to the left. Then in the second opening, she moved over one position and upwards through the middle tube. She reached the shelf and was surprised to see Sherygha standing there. Seeing the lost look on her face he explained, "I do not trust those that built for us. The temptation may get too high. So I took my time and improved the shelter. I also created a small, personal duct to get directly to the egg shelf that they do not know about." Ellydra settled into the corner they decided was the best spot and she released four eggs. The first egg was red like her father, but had a gold swirl about it. The second and third eggs were black and silver, like herself. The fourth was black and gold, like Sherygha. It would be the first time since his creation that the large male dragon saw another black dragon with gold edges.

There was but one passageway for exiting and entering near the egg shelf. It was so the dragons could leave and enter without obstacles. They made the shelf cozy for the eggs. The dragon then loosed his ice breath and closed the shelf for edge to roof. Then lay another barrier of fire. Then as they left the shelf through the upward release channel, he closed that off with ice as well. Only He or his life mate would be able to get near his first clutch.

Over the next three years, the two dragons checked on the eggs frequently. Like the cocoons the houmans stepped out of, while inside, the maturing bodies can hear the outside world. They can internalize the information, and use it once they emerge from their stasis. Ellydra would tell them her family history. She would sing the songs of the different races to them, as well as the ones dragons created. She would tell them how to be virtuous and noble like their father. Often times, she would just comment about to day, letting the growing babies learn her voice. She tried the mental connection that only dragons shared with their offspring, but she would not know if it succeeded until after they hatched. She would grab various metals and ores from her travels to add to the hoard her partner was creating. Through the thousands of years on earth, the dragons learned that consuming the metals, ores, gems and jewels of the planet not only strengthened them, but made their scales more vibrant and healthy. Not all dragons knew this, but many did, which in return made the metals more precious to both dragon kinds and humans alike.

Sherygha would stop by as well, though less often than his mate. He would bring small gems for them to eat at their awakening. He learned that in this new world, as dragons gained free will, they also became increasingly aggressive. There were more and more accounts from the dragons he knew of clutch siblings attacking each other for dominance and pecking order. That was okay with him, as it was in fact their nature, but increasingly so was the death rate of the young drakes and drakka. A clutch of five or six would be reduced to two or even one. So he told the dragons to give them a small piece of ore or gems to satisfy their need overpower. The pile was getting impressive with both parents contributing to it. The gold he retrieved, the massive dragon ate himself. The rubies, sapphires, and bronze pieces he left for his children. The silver, he gave to his dragoness.

While there, he also tried his mind link. Then he would tell of his personal history. Like his own beliefs, he wanted all his children to be wise, so he taught them everything he knew during his visits. They would not be able to put the knowledge into practice until they experienced the real world, but he hoped it would keep them virtuous in a world swiftly turning corrupt with power. He spoke of the High God and their abundance of talks. He wanted to ensure that one day, if he ever died, one or all of his children would be able to fill his position as proctor of the planet. As the wisest of the land, he could see that things were changing, but was not entirely sure it was for the better.

Then one day, while flying around Mageek, letting his scales soak up the sun on the mild fall day, he heard his love roar, loud and quick. Then another. He turned sharply, almost hitting one of the griffins following his pace. He pushed his wings hard, propelling him to the entrance of the egg shelf. He landed harshly; more nervous than any time prior in his long life. Standing behind the rocking eggs was Ellydra, beaming with joy and pride. He swiftly went back out the chute and flew towards the edge of the island where a drove of pigs were drinking their fill. He picked up a small piglet with his hind legs and a large black boar with massive arms and flew them back into the cavern shelf. He then placed them near a large puddle of water he created and froze their feet to the ground, keeping this still, but very ornery and alive. The first food his children ate was to be alive and warm. He then turned, with the animals loudly squealing in the background, and approached the now shaking eggs.

All four of them were rocking and shaking, as the baby dragons were trying to emerge from their beautiful enclosures. With a nod from Sherygha, Ellydra mind spoke to her first clutch. “Be at ease my children. As parents, this is our duty to help release you into the world." She then walked to the opposite side of her mate as they breathed the celestial power of all dragons. The egg shells slightly weakened. Then, in response, the parental dragons heard a small breaking sound. It was coming from the black and gold egg. The sole drake or drakka with their father's coloring was the first to emerge. The front claws broke through, shattering the shell holding it hostage. Then a tail with tiny bumps, soon to grow into horns, poked out the back. It reached up and swiped at the shell again. Then a nose broke through, black as night, and roared in defiance of the shell. It was a male. His first heir to reach the world was a strong male, black with gold edges like his father.

As the nose was breaking through for the black egg, the red egg seemingly shattered. A tail forcefully broke through and swung itself around the shell, smashing it as it moved. The red dragon with gold tint then put its paws between the crevice it created and forged open the enclosure. At the same time, the two black and silver dragons breached the shell as well, and began roaring with the others. Their roars were small and high, more like cries, but they were all triumphant, and proudly so.

Then, the black dashed to the red dragon, knocking it to the ground. Then he stomped his body on her arms. He was slightly larger than the other three, and knew it. After knocking down the red female, he swiped his tail at the black and silver twins, one male one female. The male fell over, while the female jumped on his back, biting at his neck. He rolled and freed himself, then attacked her, grabbing her neck and reaching around to bite her tail. She yelped in pain and growled at the largest sibling. He roared at her again, and then jumped at her, but instead of landing on her, he moved to the side. Using the tactic to catch her off guard he side swiped her with his front claws, leaving red gashes on her side. He looked around at his clutch siblings, wounded and defeated. The little black dragon walked to his red and gold sister. Still on the ground, he held his head up above her, and then tucked it below her, helping her to regain her footing. He looked around, spotting the animals still squealing in the distance. He raced towards them, but saw a sparkling coming from the left side of the floor. He instead sprinted towards the small hoard. Following the lead of the clutch winner, the other three shadowed his movements. They reached the ores and halted. Then, after giving the mound a smell, the male black and silver eat a small green gem. He shuddered as the stone fell, reaching his empty stomach, and being extracted to his scale coating. He became intoxicated by the feeling, and ate a red one too. Seeing his reaction the others did too. They ate everything there. The egg shelf champion spotted a sparkling small yellowed one. He ate it, suddenly remembering it was of the most precious metals in the world. "Gold" he said out loud. "I ate gold. It feels better than all the others. I remember now." Abruptly he looked around. He wanted to see his parents. "I know you are here," yelled the drake. "Let me see you mother, father. Please come to us."

Then mentally speaking back to them as they surveyed the floor, Ellydra said "Go eat the animals we brought you first, my dearests. Fill your stomachs with not just stones but also meat, so you will grow large and strong like your father." The newly hatched dragons raced to the pigs that were frozen there. Instinct told them to avoid the tusked one for safety. Thus, they all converged upon the piglet, tearing chunks of fresh flesh. They ate with a mad frenzy, after three years of cramped hibernation and growth. Nothing was spared of the little black and white pig. Feeling remarkably stronger, the clutch then pounced on the larger boar. Yet, older and stronger, he flayed his tusks in all directions, trying to protect itself again the hungry dragons. Through instinct, they each took turns snipping at the large beast, tiring it out. It was with a one swift lunge from the black and silver female that ended the beasts combat. She dashed under the boar while he was looking at one of her brothers, and plunged her nose horn into his throat. She then pulled it to the left and right, creating a gaping wound, and then straight up to his lower jaw. She backed away as the animal shook and grunted his last breaths, locked in place by the still frozen ice. They ate from the boar until they were satiated.

It was then the two parents dropped down from the cave roof. They each ate more parts of the beast, leaving nothing to waste. Being of full size, it was a small morsel to eat, but it still gave them strength. Licking her scaled mouth and nose, Ellydra turned to face her four children. She waited until the large male turned as well before she spoke to them. Then she said in a low, friendly tone, "I am your mother Ellydra, daughter of the red dragon Gruibi and the Green with silver, Allagira. This is your father, Sherygha. He is the strongest dragon of the world. As the protector and enforcer of this planet, all dragons fear him and his wrath. However, he is equal parts wisdom, as he is powerful. Thus learn all you can from him, from us. You will one day be the protectors of the world, and will need to use sound judgment. This is your home, the caves of Mageek. Here you will learn and train for at least three years, and then you shall unfold your wings, and take the knowledge we have given you wherever you desire. Now, Red like my father, with gold like yours, step forth Shedrya. Twins, colored like myself, come to me Ellygha and Ryghari. Lastly my clutch winner; not only strong, but courteous, and colored like your father, step forward and join your younger siblings Sherybi."

They all stood, taking in their names. Then Sherybi, the oldest and winner of the clutch yawned; and after circling, lay down to rest. The other three, much like before, followed their big brother. Then after a few moments, the egg shelf was filled with the sound of sleeping dragons. Sherygha and Ellydra were elated with four strong drakes and drakka, making a successful first clutch on their part. Still hungry, the old dragon took wing. He would bring back a large mammal for them to eat. The children would not be able to leave the cave, thus neither would his life mate, and she would need all the strength available in the upcoming months.

The years passed, and the clutch grew stronger. They learned their respective elements with a test from their father. As he took them into the woods of his island, he informed them, yet again, that the element they drew from was not hereditary. Any dragon, from any lineage could be born of any elemental power. When they reached the destination, set in a line was a pile of earth and rocks, a large bowl of water, a block of ice, and a small pillar of fire. Each of the young dragons had to walk down the system of elements, tasting the item before them. They were weary, but fear was one thing the quad had never truly known. They continued as instructed. Sherybi went first, as was the pecking order of the group. He ate a small bit of earth, and then drank a sip of water. He waited, but nothing happened. The now very large drake ate a chip of the ice and moved towards the fire when he precipitously stopped. He felt a twinge of higher power than the ordinary one they all shared and mastered growing up. The feelings were like a mountain, stored in his body, now released and open to be used. Looking around, he noticed how sharp his eyes became. Suddenly, he could hear everything down to the small flying insects. He was more aware of each sense of his body, and became enthralled by it. His dragon ancestor memories kicked in and now suddenly longed to fly. Sherybi ran to a tree, his almost serpentine drake body keeping low to the ground. He climbed it upwards and roared. The roar was not a tenth as powerful as his father, but it still sent flocks of birds retreating and animals scurrying out of harm's way. It was still a long way to go, but the young black and gold dragon knew that he was powerful, and thanks to the foresight of his parents, wise as well. He puffed up some air, held it, broadening his already wide chest and blew out the ice of his birthright. Though only a small cool breath was the final effect, it was still more than before.

The other dragons were leaping towards the tests when Sherygha told them to behave and wait their turns. As was the order amongst the group, the black and silver female, Ryghari went next. She did not have to wait.

As soon as she swallowed the earth she felt the same rush of power. Then she ran off to attack her ice brother. The red drakka, Shedrya, daintily walked over, taking her demeanor from her mother, and swiftly ate the rocks. She stood tall and proud, and waited. However, nothing happened to the red. She just as delicately walked to the water and took a large gulp. She again paused for the effect. Yet still, nothing happened. She laughed and went to the ice and bit off a large piece, somewhat more unceremoniously. She thought she felt something. She stirred and looked around. However, it was not her elemental power rushing to her, but the sudden cold of the ice. She stammered about and filled her mouth with the acidic saliva from her bile sacs to rid herself of the hammering cold. Once feeling better she forgot about decorum and jumped to the fire. She inhaled the smoke. She held it, but soon released it, coughing as well. All four elements were not of her nature. She was puzzled. Her father laughed at the show from his red daughter. He told her to look behind the fire at the small swirling wind an Ormaque set for him. She did and walked to it. He told her to inhale it and feel its power. While she was walking, Ellygha the male twin went through the process. When he reached fire, he also got dizzy with power. His eyes and ears narrowed and he filled with pride and power. He spit his acid at his red and gold sibling. As it left his mouth, it burst into flames. It was a liquid fire to the young dragons. Shedrya jumped out of the way and into the wind. It looked light, but was strong enough to toss the drakka to her side; though she did not mind, being it was the opposite area of her brother's attack. She sucked in some of the swirling air. She held it, and then blew back at the small black male like her ancestor memories showed her. But it was nothing but regular breath.

Confused and sad, the child ran to her father for comfort. All three of the other siblings had powers, yet she did not. She could not fathom why she would be the only dragon to not receive the powers of the planet. She began to weep. Sad for his daughter and also a bit perplexed at the situation the dragon quickly came up with a solution. It was one that in fact, made him let out a soft purr. He rubbed his daughter with his tail as he spoke to her, "Do not fret my ruby. Like your body color, you stand out and differ from your siblings. So your power is just as strong as fire, but yet rarer. The sixth element, if you remember… is lightning. I in all honesty, did not even think to find a way to bring it for you young ones. It is so rare that there are very few of this world who wields it. However, your mother's mother was a holder of lightning, so it has been passed down to you. Just as your color comes from her father, you are the perfect mix of your mother's parents. So my young princess, tonight, after we eat, I will fly you to a storm. With the lightning surrounding us, you will be able to consume it like your clutch brethren. Then forever the power will reside within you." She lay there with her massive father. She was undoubtedly, the most feminine of the young group. Much like her mother, she was sleek and smooth with a thin graceful neck and long serpentine tail. Sherygha was always reminded of how much she physically took after her mother Ellydra. Her body and demeanor was simply a wingless shadow of his mate. He was very happy to have such wonderful heirs. He decided it was time to move away. He blew ice over the fire and water. Then fire over the ice and earth. He instructed his children to smash the tests and then follow him for another hunting trip.

That evening, after all were fed, he headed to the exit with the small red. Ellydra, already informed of the day's earlier events, bade them safe journeys. The two left he cave. He went high above the lake, outstretched his wings to catch a waft of air and floated. He sniffed moving air above in various directions but could not smell a storm. Therefore he knew that he would have to travel east of the enchanted lake towards the grand ocean. Over the ocean were a multitude of storms. Most were created by nature, some by wind and water dragons having duels, or simply having fun. Most dragons, unless born of the water component, did not venture too far into the raging ocean. It was an arduous task for one to return home if suddenly swept into the harsh storms that brewed over the watery mass. Therefore, the black dragon was not entirely happy about making the trip, especially since he would be carrying his daughter with him. Nevertheless, it was a promise he intended to keep. He grabbed the red dragon and launched into the air. He beat his enormous wings with force, gaining large amounts of altitude. He would allow the air to carry them as much as possible, saving his strength and energy to navigate the storm and make their way back towards land.

Sherygha had forgotten how long the trip was. He only planned to leave that night, and return by the next afternoon. However, it was a day's flight when flew steadily. Allowing the wind to coast him and his daughter there would take a day and a half, almost two. So twice he settled, allowing the young one to walk on land, and eat. He would not feed her though, as she was now almost two years of age, she could hunt smaller game for herself. This was the perfect test to see if she could manage outside of the island and the forest on the other side of the lake. He looked at her, softly stalking a brown rabbit. It had not noticed her until she decided to change positions. No longer downwind from the prey, it picked up her distinct dragon scent and scurried away. Shedrya gave chase to the live prey. It was her nature. The fat rabbit hopped left and then right. It was frantic with outwitting the giant predator. Even though the drakka was not quite two years of age, she was already the size of a jaguar at her body, and as long as a large snake from nose horn to tail. She jumped from spot to spot in response to the fleeing meal. Then she decided to take the offensive and lashed out her tail. It moved too fast for the furry rabbit to acknowledge its forthcoming. With a hard smack, the rabbit was sent into a small tree. Dazed and unable to flee anymore, Shedrya pounced on the rabbit, biting into its neck until suffocation. Then she drove her small nose horn into its white belly and ripped it open. She ate the nutrient rich delicacy of the liver, intestines, spleen, and heart first. Then she began scraping the fur off while her father brought down a large horned herbivore. He also ate the insides and a side of the ribs and lungs, and then carried the remainder of the large meal to the group of carnivorous predators waiting in the grass. She ate the rabbit whole as her father approached her. She was not fully satisfied, but it would hold. Then, fully knowing his daughter, she saw her father brought her a thick leg from his prey to feed her. She wolfed it down quickly and the two set off again.

As they flew, Shedrya took in all the sights and sounds. It was all new to her, and yet familiar. Her father told her that his and her mother's memories, as well as her grandparents' memories were inside of her. So even though she is experiencing the world for the first time, she will never be lost. Shedrya loved learning from her father. He seemed to know everything. Her mother often referred to him as the wisest of all the earthly species, and talking with him made her believe it more and more every time. Though she had heard the story many times from her mother, she never heard her father's telling of how they met, danced and mated. Thus, she asked her father, "Would a great dragon such as you be inclined to tell his daughter how he won my mother while on this voyage?" This made the gliding dragon laugh loudly. He lost altitude and had to beat his wings to pick up the pace again. "You even speak like your mother, using such flattery on an old dragon," he answered. "You are like a red version of her, prodding the better part of me to do your bidding. Ha ha ha, well seeing as how we have some time in the air left, I will indulge you my beautiful daughter." Then the dragon told his daughter of how he met, won and danced with her mother. It was the first time he ever told anyone about the encounter with Ellydra's father since he spoke with Rynesch years before. He also asked Shedrya to never reveal his treachery to her mother or clutch siblings, for that would disengage their image of him and cause her great pain.

As he finished the recounting asked of him, they reached the shore of the ocean. They landed and watched the dawn rise together in silence. It was a moment between father and daughter than needed no words. He stood there, towering above his lovely red and gold daughter and sent not a mental conversation but a feeling. *I love you, little one*. She purred at the warm feeling and laid her tail across his.

When the sun was fully up, Sherygha sniffed the salty air. As he predicted, a storm was coming inward swiftly. He opened his wings, letting his daughter know it was time to leave. He grabbed her and flapped his wings hard and steady, aiming straight for the incoming tempest. After obtaining a few miles over the water the wind began whipping against them harshly. He pulled the red dragon to his chest, covering her with his massive arms and pushed against the wind and rain. He was immersed in the raging storm and already wanting to leave. He had to be cautious not to be struck by a flying by lightning dragon. Or by the true lightning itself. He turned his body upward, pointed his nose to heavens and tail to the cold salty water below. Then he motioned his wings as powerful as he could; launching him to the highest points of the storm. Amidst the rolling clouds there was a brewery of lightning. With water and wind beating against him, he intertwined his tail and Shedrya's. Then he put her atop his large back. He went closer to the charging lightning streaks that he could see behind the thundering clouds. It may be a risk by doing so, but he had to allow his daughter to eat the bolts as promised. Also, he was sure that if he happened to be struck by the powerful surge, he would survive, though very painfully.

He stayed in the angry dense clouds trying to get near a swift moving bolt. He was taking the nature's abuse in stride. The dragon had set his mind, and he would not let his daughter down. Then as he turned left to catch a massive amount of charges his daughter was knocked off his back, taking the scales she was gripping with her, by a strong gust of wind and water. He tried to balance himself and go after the dragon, but just as she was falling over, a strong bolt of lightning struck the dragons. When it ended, he mentally told his daughter to hold on and try to internalize the element. However, as soon as he finished he was barraged with three more shocks back to back. Stunned and shaking, Sherygha's wings buckled and the dragon's began falling. The free fall seemed to last longer than one earth year as he tried to hold on to his child. He was twirling around like the winds around him. He drastically wanted to reach Shedrya, but the momentum of the fall and the stoic muscles, still shocked and immobile, would not allow him to. Besides his tail, increasingly loosening as they reached the water below, he had no connection to her.

Sherygha focused his will, pulling from all strength he had left. Using the only motion he could muster, he threw his daughter above him right before he broke the water's rampant surface. With the lack of momentum and gravity, the splash would not crush his young daughter. He already knew it was very possible he would not die. Dragons could breathe underwater like the amphibians of the planet, though they preferred not to. Thus, one of the worst things that would happen to him would be that he entered into a watery hibernation until he floated ashore, got found by a water dragon, or healed and awoke on his own merit. However, while down there, it was more likely that a creature would get through his scales and then could eat him alive or poison and kill him without any chance of being able to stop them. Thinking about his possible fates as he drifted downward he looked up through his water slits and saw his red daughter break the surface. She stirred, meaning she had not died upon impact. Knowing the fact that his offspring still stood a chance to survive the ordeal, he slowly drifted to the watery bottom with a restored state of mind. He tried sending one more mind connection and told his possible last words. "Remember all I have taught you my sweet child. Swim to shore, tap into your dragon memories to find the safest way home and relay the events to Ellydra and your siblings. Then once your wings grow strong, you and your siblings must find a man named Shaman and tell him of my fate as well. I love you, my beautiful Shedrya." He ended the mind link and closed his eyes. With his senses stupefied he could not recall how far he drifted before he hit the ocean bed. Yet, he did realize that he was no longer spiraling downward. "So this to be it" he thought. "This salty floor, filled with low water creatures will be the place of my burial. How shameful. Please forgive me Father, I earnestly tried." Then everything, first being a haze, went black and silent for the protector of the world.

WREAKING HAVOC

Ellydra had become troubled to the point of shakes. She did not want to leave her young children, with wings still growing in the sacs on their back. However, her mate and daughter had not returned in just over three months. She feared the worse for her sweet natured daughter, but could not fathom what could bring down the giant Sherygha. She made up her mind and told her remaining brood her resolve. "I will be leaving for a couple of days to gather information. During this time you all will stay on the egg shelf. I will bring you two large bulls to eat, as well as stones for your scales. Stand at the edge of the open chute to allow some sun to grace your bodies. Sherybi, you take care of your siblings these few days in my stead. I will return shortly." She then turned and headed to the main tunnel.

Finishing what she promised to her children, Ellydra departed Mageek and headed east to the ocean like her mate and daughter had done three months prior. As she neared the edge of the lake, a frequent visitor and friend was nearing her. She slowed to speak to the frantic black dragon. Yet, when they reached each other she could see Ellydra was not the same. After a quick discussion, the blue and emerald dragoness named Mifawr decided she would aid the black dragon on her journey. They departed the area, flying as quickly as they could.

They traveled for many miles, surveying the land beneath them. After a day and a half with little food besides the occasional passing bird they decided to rest their wings and eat. They landed in an area with an abundance of herding creatures. Each of the dragons caught one of the grazing animals to feast on. In the middle of eating they both caught the scents of the horrible smelling Arfaet race. It must have been travelers because not many individuals of that race lived in this area, generally occupied by Norfex or a few Mylare in the trees. They stalked to higher ground, staying out of sight of the barbaric people. They were indeed a travelling caravan. They wore scales for armor and again horns and teeth for weapons as well as ornaments. There was no mistaking the warriors of the arfaet people. Not all were blood thirsty murderers, as she later realized, but many were and the warriors more than the rest. They had three cages holding various animals under a tent. The confinement was made from wood the bones of an enormous animal. A whale or the larger of the dragon species was most likely the one that had its bones taken. Wanting nothing more to do with the dragon butchers, Ellydra turned away to return to her meal. However, before she could move four paces Mifawr quietly spoke aloud, “One of the captures is a young red dragon. Looking at the tail edge and size I don’t even think they have released their wings from their casings. Even though, I will admit, with the wounds on it I cannot be sure. Come back and look my friend. Is that your red Shedrya?” Ellydra became so overcome with anxiety she jumped back atop to rock, almost giving away their presence to the brutal nomads as a few rocks stumbled down. She peered deep at the tail, and then sniffed the air. It was too shaded to see and too distant to truly acquire a good enough smell to be sure amidst the stink of the Arfaet. Then, she suddenly remembered, the mind link. "Is that you, my dear Shedrya?" asked the hopeful dragoness. "If it is my sweet red daughter, lift your tail for two seconds, turn it to the right and then pull it inside the tent." She waited a few moments as they moved by at a snail's pace. She, needing it be her missing daughter, closed her eyes and mentally spoke the same exact words again. She then told Mifawr what she asked the young dragon to do, so she could see if there was a response as well. There was none. The black dragon let out a soft whimper. She stood tall, not caring about being seen since the convoy was almost past them. She directed he mind, thinking solely about her beautiful red and gold daughter, lowered her head and said it a third time. She looked up and right as they were heading around a bend the little tail was pointed upward. The blue dragon tapped her, seeing the same thing. Then the tail turned right. The two dragons were both standing now, hearts racing in anticipation of the final step. They took a step or two backwards and stopped breathing when the tail slowly disappeared inside the tent covering. It was her daughter, still alive and captured by the same ruffian race that accosted her father and killed her mother.

Before she realized it, Ellydra had taken flight. As she neared the group she roared loud and hateful. She flew from the back to the front, releasing not only her flame, but the burning spit as well. The mortals below had stopped, now scattering and calling to arms. She did not recognize any of the faces, but it mattered not, they wore armor forged of dragon scales, and were thus, an enemy. The black dragon yelled down to the flaming area, "My wonderful drakka. Tell me you are not on your last breaths. I am coming to rescue you." She dipped onto the first caravan, tearing apart the wooden boards and planks. The man driving slashed at her vital, unscaled neck. He had his opportunity and lost it. As his arm was on the downswing, the dragon bit down on her opponent, ripping his head from its body. When she gulped the head a spear hit her scale. It simply loosened it and bounced off, but added to her fury nonetheless. She took to the sky again and released her fire for a second time. They all ducked for cover. She landed, able to move faster on the ground, dashed to the jail holding her offspring and knocked it down with her tail and legs. Another man loudly yelped. She looked to her right and saw the blue dragon wreaking havoc on the hindmost participants of the procession. A fast moving one jumped away from her and in one motion pulled out his blade. He was running towards the dragon and would have severely wounded her as he was in her blind spot while she fought two men. He was within a couple of yards when a roar came through and a bolt of lightning struck the assailant. She looked where it came from, and saw her daughter, badly beaten and scarred. The scales had not grown back correctly where some gashes had badly healed. The beautiful red drakka would now be forever blemished by the Arfaet monsters. Seeing her daughter sick, injured and small from not eating adequately, Ellydra's vehemence peaked. She had never been this angry. The time of her mother's death, or the fight against the men using her own father's scales to do battle with her were nothing compared to the fury smoldering in the black dragon at the mistreatment of her daughter. She beat her wings hard, pushing her swiftly to the sky and then did a nose dive back to the surface. She approached the nearing ground and rained down fire on the remaining cavalcade below. Mifawr grabbed the barely walkable drakka and hastened away from the increasing inferno. One younger arfaet woman was running from the blaze, clothes scorching as fast as she could run. She rolled on ground to quell her burning. She then reached the Mifawr and Shedrya and fell to her knees, begging them to spare her life. Ellydra, eyes filled with rage, landed heavily behind the pleading blonde haired woman. She answered tightly, trying to control her voice, "Tell me why I should not put my nose horn through your chest and let my daughter devour your body. And believe me when I say it had better be a GRAND reason mortal, for I am not feeling very lenient at the moment."

"I did not mistreat your daughter," replied the sobbing teenager through haggard breaths. "When my father found her, she was near unconscious. He was going to kill her right then, but I convinced him to spare her life by telling him she was not yet a full dragon and could be worth more at a later time. She doesn't even have wings yet. So my brother and I then tended to her oh beautiful one. I often times would even feed her more rations than I was ordered so she could build some strength, even if slowly. Also, when alone, we three would talk about many things too. Please, I beg you, do not kill me. I was not your daughter's enemy, and I am not your enemy. I consider her my closest friend"

The weak red drakka spoke up for the first time since the rescue. "She is not being false mother. Of all the people on the caravan, she and her younger brother were the only ones who showed any concern for me. I would be dead if she had not stopped her father and uncles from killing me, even if she could not stop the daily torturing. She really is my friend." Then she turned away and looked east, the direction of the ocean.

"Mother," continued Shedrya, "are we going to the ocean to find my father? He took multiple hits of lightning before becoming paralyzed and plummeting into the ocean below. But I know where he is. I was trying to gain strength to go retrieve him when I was captured. I was still entirely too weak to fight back." She looked down and softly added, "I'm so sorry I let you down."

The black dragon walked over to her daughter and rested her arm on her swollen and tortured back. She sent celestial healing power into her daughter. The Blue and emerald dragon followed suit. After a few moments, and seeing some of the large wounds heal better, she spoke to her young one. "When your wings are released from the pouches on your back you will also gain a power that allows you to heal yourself and others. It will allow you to summon hidden strength. It will allow you to tap into your memories at any moment instead of extreme cases. So no, I am not disappointed in you my dear. You are still a child. In fact, in dragon terms, you are still an infant. You are just simply not equipped to do what you desired. Nevertheless, you have survived their abuse and are able to show me where your father is. I even saw you shock the Arfaet man with a bolt of lightning. I am truly the proudest mother there could ever be. Now rest for the night you children. I will keep the young female with us so she does not suffer harm from any predator animals of the night. Tomorrow I will send her on her way while we retrieve my dragon love." Ellydra then flew off for an hour. When she returned she noticed that Mifawr doused the raging fire with her water. Though she brought back food, Ellydra saw the red drakka and her sole companion during for the past months were nuzzled together, asleep. It was then that the black and silver dragon saw the markings of abuse on the mortal teenager as well. Showing compassion for her injured daughter apparently brought abuse on the mortal as well. She put down the limp animal and then gestured to the injuries with her tail, showing Mifawr. The other dragon nodded in acknowledgement. They poured a small amount of heavenly energy into the mortal, healing a score of untreated wounds that her own people inflicted on her, as well as the burns she received while fleeing. She woke the duo, prodding them to eat the fresh caught food. She took the lower part of the leg and cooked it for the blonde female, and then tossed the remaining corpse to her daughter. Mifawr had built a great hunger during the skirmish. So while the young ones were eating she migrated to the wreckage. Underneath one of the tents was a baby elephant, only burnt on the outside. So the blue female broke through the brittle and scorched bones and carried out the contents. She opened up the mid-section and ate the smoky tasting insides. Then she began eating the fatty meat of the elephant after tearing off the blackened flesh. Ellydra floated over and joined the meal. She knew that she would need to replenish her energy to complete the next task of rescuing her life mate from the ocean floor. Afraid of leaving he daughter alone, she returned to her red drakka and finished eating the muscular and meaty tusk. As the red fell back asleep, the black dragon extended her wings, covering the young dragon and arfaet girl for the night.

The next morning, Shedrya was spry and hunting small field rodents. Though, having a limp made her fairly unsuccessful. She kept trying though. Her body was weak but her spirit was as strong as any of her other children. Then after about thirty minutes, right before she was going to depart to search for Sherygha, she changed her tactics. She crouched down, much like before, and while a healthy sized green snake was slithering across the plains she opened her mouth and sent a small bolt to the legless creature. It shook and trembled, then lay still, shocked motionless, but still alive. Shedrya was elated at being able to kill again after months of inactivity. She grabbed the snaked and bit off half its body, delighting in every bite. Then she finished off the serpent and headed to her mother. She saw a severe look of concern on black dragon's scaled face. Then the realization of what today entailed flooded into the red dragons mind, which in turn, made her remember all of the events that led up to that point. It would be an eventful day. Luckily, there was no storm this time thought the healing drakka.

"Let us depart," spoke the mother dragon. "We have much ground to cover, and I have to carry you." Then in a mind link, "I'm truly glad you are getting back to your old self my sweet Shedrya." She then grabbed her daughter and flew towards the ocean, the blue dragon and blond haired girl following closely behind.

They reached the area that Sherygha and Shedrya entered the storm. Hovering above the water they tried looking down through the moving water. With no luck, Ellydra dropped her daughter into the water and went in behind her. She told her daughter to show her where he was through a mind connection, but to stay near the surface in case she needs a swift retreat. Then she dived towards the floor. Looking down, the red drakka told her to move left and go straight down.

As she descended she wondered if her mate was still alive. She pushed downward trying to get there as fast as she could, when to her right she saw a large lump protruding from the ground and out of place. It was a large hill in the middle of a sandy edge surrounded with algae and small shellfish. She swam to the mass. With her tail she wiped a section clear. There was a collection of gold scales shining back at her. In a panic she began removing the ocean's sandy floor with a fury. She needed to see that he was alive. She needed to hear him roar. She needed him to say some witty comment. Plain and simple, she needed him. She uncovered most of the top of the dragon when she saw her daughter and friend appear. The three uncovered the unmoving giant. They each grabbed a part of the dragon, and swam for the surface. It was a slow retreat due to the mass of the dead weight. They finally breached the surface of the water, and still needed to take him some miles inward to land. It was decided that the red dragon would guide them and the two adult dragons would propel them. Mifawr was in the water, and Ellydra was above. They both released their power in a steady stream. The water dragon pushed the body from the water, while the fire dragon let her fire move them forward. Thus, the drakka had the most important job, to ensure they reach land. After three steady bursts of power, they were on the sandy shore. Tired and anxious, the group looked upon Sherygha. The giant dragon still did not stir. They tried everything to awaken the colossal lump. Ellydra could not believe her misfortune. Her life mate was laying here, dead. And more than that, Sherygha, the proctor of the world, here to ensure balance and order no longer breathed. It was too much for the dragon. She went into water, weeping loudly. After a few minutes of dealing with her grief, she walked to the unmoving dragon. Looking to the sky she roared, full of sorrow and despair, but got no response. She then softly spoke to her deceased mate, "Please my love, say my name one more time before you leave me." Then she placed her head on his horned crown and wept some more.

"I went through great lengths to learn that name Ellydra," answered the static dragon in a breathy whisper. "And for what you had me do, I shall not stop saying it just yet." He opened one eye, seeing his mate standing back and looking on with unsure hope. So the dragon slowly stood. He looked at his mate square in the eyes and said, stronger than before, "I am the strongest dragon of the land. Your eyes do not deceive you my love. I am back from my hibernation. I truly thank you three for retrieving me from the watery depths." The dragon shook his body, trying to release some lodged sand and shelled mollusks that the Ormaques sometimes ate. He then stomped his arms down, cocked his head forward and to the ocean and roared loudly in defiance. Keeping his promise to his daughter had almost taken his life. He looked at her with pleasure as only she could have known where to bring his mate to save him. Then he became aware the many bruises on his young drakka. She hid behind her mother as she realized what he was looking at. He shifted backwards, turning his head away from his daughter. It was his fault that his beautiful red daughter was now scarred for life. If he could have held on a little longer he would have been able to spare her the anguish he knows she felt. The young species could be so loving; but could also be cruel and barbaric. And the level of cruelty could know no bounds with some races. Sherygha did not need to know her exact ordeal. By seeing the aftermath of the torture, he could already vividly imagine the process. It was the fact that she was still alive and not deceased with her red and gold scales being used for armor that brought some joy to the tired dragon.

He turned again and saw the human girl with blonde hair. Not particularly fond of the species at that moment, he crouched low, growled and began moving towards the arfaet girl. He swelled up, ready to release a power that could have put a crater in the ground. However, before he could release it on the child that was with the group the blue and emerald dragon jumped in front of him and roared at him. Sherygha, fury high, did not recognize the dragon at first, but right before he decided to kill them both he saw that it was not some Arfaet friendly dragon, but their friend, Mifawr. He was confused. He shook his head, as hopes of clearing his understanding. His graceful mate walked over and bit the massive dragon's tail. He turned to his mate and spoke low, "What is going on, my love? I know why she is scarred and bruised, but I am not able to understand why we are harboring an Arfaet child. I do not allow many to devour humans, but we should end her life immediately."

Ellydra answered sweetly and loudly for the entire party to hear. "I as well as you am indebted to this… *Arfaet* child. She was the only member of the caravan that captured our sweet daughter that showed her compassion and mercy. In fact, when her father was just about to kill her, this little one talked him into sparing her life. If you look closely, that tenderness came at a price as well. So if this smelly girl is the sole reason our sweet Shedrya is still alive, then we shall also take care of her. I have spared her life, and she will accompany us to Mageek. I suppose she will be able to live amongst the Ormaques."

Sherygha shook his head and responded as he slowly lifted off the ground, "She is allowed to stay among us, but not with the Ormaques. She will stay in the cave and the third island unless we accompany her." Then, directing his attention to the cowering girl he said, "You have done me a great service young one. You will be raised as a tender to our young dragons. Not slavery, but service. I cannot allow you to leave often, as I have seen the ways of your species, more importantly your Arfaet race. Thus I cannot endanger my cluster cave." After seeing her saddened face he turned and slowly added,

"However, earn my trust over these next few years, and then we shall negotiate the standings at which you have been accepted. Come all, I wish to see my other children and rest at the cave of my design."

The large black and gold dragon went to his cavern at Mageek. They lived there for the next few years. Even though the arfaet teenager was used as a dragon tender, she enjoyed being around the dragons. She was allotted a medium sized room and almost every luxury she asked for. It was not a bad life. She at times longed for more human companionship, but growing up on a caravan with blood thirsty men, always destroying dragons and people alike, was the worst kind of life she could think of. She dedicated her life to the dragons, and they loved her in return; especially the red drakka Shedrya. After a year back at home, they realized that the red drakka would never fully open her wings. On her back the slimy casings grew, just like her siblings, but when they broke free, they were stunted and deformed. It was the side effect of her father and uncles stabbing and cutting her across the spine when they were angry or filled with ale.

The red dragon Shedrya opened her wings as much as possible. It shook and crackled as she tried to flap them in place. "This is wrong" she solemnly thought to herself. She was at the top of the egg shelf exit. Her siblings were flying around freely and learning their wings while she sat there watching... sadly. She was not able to fly. Not able to truly become a dragoness, master of land, sea and most importantly, sky. She thought about all of the dreams she used to have, flying over the land and striking enemies with lightning. How ironic it was, that the rarest of all elements was given to her, and she would never properly use it.

Frustrated and driven to prove fate wrong, she simply jumped off the edge of the cliff and outstretched her worrisome wings. It was an exhilarating experience. She could not flap her wings swiftly or with force, but she could in fact move them enough to ride the overlaying breezes. Thus, hope was not lost to her. She would still not fly over the land like other dragons, but she would not live her life enclosed in the same cave she was born in. As she neared the ground she heard cheers of approval coming from her circling siblings. Waiting at the mountain entrance was Vora, the now seventeen year old Arfaet girl that bonded with the red drakka.

"Vora," Shedrya said excitedly, "I took to the sky. I could not fly, but I soared down on the wind. Did you see? Please tell me you saw me with my wings out! Was I glorious? I am no longer a drakka now that I took flight. I am a full DRAGONESS! I am so happy. Tell me, was I beautiful like my mother?"

Vora answered excitedly, "Yes, my queen. You were absolutely glorious. I will go into town and inform your parents that you wish to speak with them after their meeting with Shaman and the others on the elder council." She sprinted into the woods of the third island to reach the dragons parents. When she did, her breath was heavily panting as she told the congregation of the unexpected feat.

Ellydra opened her wings and took to the sky to locate her daughter, uncaring of anything else. Sherygha bade Shaman a swift farewell and safe voyage back to the other lake they had inhabited. He reminded him to ensure they all stuck to what he taught them as the miniature cloister began to grow, and he looked forward to the monthly updates. Then he, with Vora in his clutches, followed his mate to meet their daughter who just defied fate with a single leap and her undying spirit.

A BOY ON THE RUG

As **Shaman flew back towards** the second lake home, he felt at peace. In wyvern form he could feel close to the dragons in the sky. Every month the powerful Ormaque would fly back to report to Sherygha, but sometimes he would travel to various regions of Choi. This day, he decided he would see a region that he did not visit as often as he should. It was the homeland of the Hufore. Once a few years back while in wyvern form he flew to meet the one person of the species that he knew was wiser than himself. Shaman saw she was entertaining a group of olive skinned Arfaet and decided to keep his distance until they left. He landed a distance away and transformed into a wolf. He stalked the campsite from the remoteness of the sparse trees and high grass that thrived between the settlement and the forest. As he approached the site he saw the man pull out a blade and stab the queen. Then, he sadly witnessed the massacre of the ones left in the village. Right as he decided he would have to fight the barbarians to save the children a small drakka descended upon him. She was young, not even a year judging by the length of her horns. Shaman, in werewolf form howled loudly at the drakka. Three times larger than a normal wolf would be; he was a great deal larger than the young dragon female. Looking back towards the village, he saw the large man looking in their direction. He jumped towards the green and pearl drakka. They battled for minutes. Shaman was larger and stronger, but the dragon was faster and lithe. They swapped claws and bruises. The dragon was well aware of its tail and smacked the grey werewolf across the face, sending him into a tree. The dragon dashed towards him but Shaman bit down on her leg, breaking it. Then he tossed her into a prickly bush. It cut into her unshielded neck, causing a flow of blood to be opened. The dragon righted herself, but could not fully stand with the bones of her arm shattered from the heavy bite. Shaman, knowing full well how much Sherygha hated his species killing dragons, left the losing drakka to tend to herself.

He dashed to the now burning village. Everything was aflame. He ran around, trying to see if any children had been left behind, but there were none. He was going to pay respects to the dead queen when he suddenly realized she was not there either. It was peculiar. He vividly saw the large man stab her in this very spot, but there was no trace of her. Shaman shifted back to human form and looked around. He took some water and sprayed it over the area, putting out some flames. Then he looked again and could see the red trail of blood leading around to the back of the burning shelter. There was a mound of dirt with a foot sticking out. He shape shifted again to a large badger with huge paws for digging. He quickly dug the queen out and felt her soft breaths. She was not yet dead. And wow, she was also beautiful. The stark features of her face were a contrast to the smooth curves of her body. Her hands were soft and delicate. Her lips curved along and her hair was the soft like air and the color of the sunset. How could the brute destroy such beauty?

Shaman glimmered into a wyvern and grabbed the dying queen. He went to the forest edge where the broken dragon had scooted to and was still laying. He dropped the queen off gently next to her and shifted back into his normal form. He took out a vial of water he always kept full from the mystical lake that was his original home. Pouring the water over the queen first, and the dragon second, he decided he would heal both at the same time. He weaved the water through the wounds with his hands and mind. He put the bones back together for the dragon's arm. The queen had already removed the blade from her abdomen. So he first used the water to clean the dirt from the wound, and then repaired her insides and closed the hole. It would be sore for months, but if the blood loss was not too much already, she would live. Then he closed the large wound the dragon's neck. Using his power to extreme limits, the man drank the last few drops of water he brought from Lake Mageek, and collapsed.

He awoke what felt like hours later inside of a cave. The queen was sitting next to him. She was alive and alert, but her beautiful face was masked behind an unfathomable sadness. Shaman looked around and took in the surroundings. It was a vast cave, with very high ceilings. It held piles of gems and pretty stones that dragons ate to revitalize and strengthen their almost impenetrable scales all over the cave. There were bats flying around, so he knew it had to be night. A fire was in the corner and some small animal was cooking over it. Above the fire and to the right was a shelf. So Shaman realized they had not been kidnapped by someone from the Uckleet, but a dragon. Then as he looked around some more he saw the young green and pearl drakka blending in with the moss and cave in a dark corner. She realized he was looking at her and stood, as tall as he was. Walking over to the two people, she spoke softly, "You two are here, at my egg cave. Two clutch brothers killed each other when they first hatched. Three months later my parents died trying to protect us from the stink people like you. We were able to hide due to our small sizes and the dark, hidden holes of the cave. Then, while out hunting for food, my last brother broke his leg and got trampled by the stampede he was stalking. It was only my sister and I living in this large home made for us. Then, little over two months ago, my sister fell asleep at the edge while trying to get sun on her scales. She fell over." Tears puddled her hazel eyes. "We were not even a year old, so there were no wings to help her. She broke her neck and the animals below consumed her body. I have been on my own ever since. When I attacked the large wolf, it was because I was afraid that it was going to attack me first. However, I lost. I thought I was going to be eaten but to my surprise I awoke to you healing me and another female of your species with only water. So I brought you both back here, to safety. You are very kind. So I have saved you, as you have saved me."

Queen Zharda then spoke softly, "You have been asleep for three days. Please eat the food the dragon has brought for us. Thank you for saving my life. I wish I could stand and join you at the fire, but it seems that when the brute stabbed me, he damaged something and I can no longer walk on my own free will."

Shaman stood and hoisted up the queen too. He took her to the meal area and then sat her against the wall. He fed her some food and sat beside her. While they ate, they talked about many things. Zharda was sad, sending her entire clan away, then losing her husbands and staff before her very eyes, and now she finds out that the very same men that used and attacked her village, abducted her children.

They talked and lived at the cave for the next few weeks. They spoke about many things, much like he originally wanted to do. However, when he felt at full strength, he decided it was time he left. He told the dragon and the queen that he would periodically stop by to check on them, but he had other responsibilities that must be kept. The queen asked the Ormaque man to stay the night and leave in the morning. Seeing the pleading in the beautiful round black eyes of this queen he answered, "Of course I will your majesty. How could I deny one such as you?" He stroked her sunset hair, filling her with warm sensations.

That night, the Zharda drug her body to the sleeping Shaman. She woke him with a kiss and began touching him over his body. She whispered in his ear, "Please indulge me this night. I have been so lonely. I have no kinsmen or birth home. I no longer have any husbands, or even children. There is only comfort from you and the young dragon, and she cannot fill certain voids in my life. I am a female, more than any other title, and I fear the loneliness that will settle once you leave. Be mine this night, noble and handsome Shaman. Please." The two embraced each other and then spent the night mating with each other. It was the first time for the Ormaque. He enjoyed every minute of the tantalizing experience. Then in the morning, he hunted a deer for the two females in the cave so they would not have to worry about food for a day or two. Then he shifted into a wyvern and went to the new lake he, and his group inhabited.

Now visiting was always a cause for joy and sadness at seeing the crippled beautiful queen. Over the past few years she had gotten stronger, but still could not walk. He had always wanted to move the queen to his home at the cloister. However the distance would be too great for him to carry her alone. The dragon was willing to help, but it was still too early to introduce a dragon to the still growing village-market.

He entered the cave in normal form. However this time was different. He heard screaming and ran inside. There on the cave floor lay a rug of wool. And atop the rug was a sitting baby, with brown skin and auburn hair. He smiled at the Hufore baby, but as he approached the infant he saw something that distressed him highly. His eyes were not black like the queen, but purple, like the Ormaque. The queen had now given him more than just physical comfort. She had now given him a child, a male heir. Zharda had given him a baby male of his own lineage that he can teach and raise to use his power to help the world as well.

"Shamanul, be with ease on the wool rug, my son. I cannot move as fast as you my dear one." Zharda was pulling her lame body from a corner of the cave as she addressed her youngest son. The baby looked at his mother and giggled. Then he stood and began walking towards his mother. The Ormaque was in awe. Had he been away so long that he not only had a child but one old enough to walk.

Shaman spoke to queen, “I came to visit you again, and saw this boy on a rug. He has purple eyes like my people. So I am sure that he is my son. However, I do not remember you seeming with child. Have I neglected you that long my dear Zharda.”

“I was in fact with child, but as the last time you visited was late, we did not leave the shelter as is our tradition. So you could not see the swell of my belly. Almost two months after your visit our sweet dragon helped me give birth to our son. I named him after you so he would always know his father’s name. He is smart and beautiful, like us.” After a silence from the man she continued, “Are you happy? I am truly sorry I did not tell you when you visited. You were so tired and the comfort from mating put my mind elsewhere. Then you were sleep and gone in the morning. Our dragon, Lypara, wanted to go after you, but her wings are fresh and not as fast as you in the wyvern form.

“Now our son is six months of age and can already walk and speak. He is smarter than any of my other children.” At the mention of the children she lost to the Arfaet, Prince Pluvach, Zharda began to softly weep. Shaman walked over and comforted the queen of the Hufore race. He spoke softly in her ear while the child played, “I will bring you and our family to the growing village market. I cannot tell anyone that you are alive, but from this day, I will be yours, my queen. I cannot bring back the children you lost, but I will form a new clan with you. Together, we will create a family that works closer with dragons to help each other grow in this beautiful world. I will not show them young Lypara just yet, but I will create the same spell we use to hide Mageek and give her a cave to grow in. My son will be yours alone, but I will check on my loves as often as possible. I promise you this, my queen." He knelt further in front of the sitting Zharda, waiting her approval. She laughed and patted his head.

She responded with a broad smile, "You will be my last and only husband. Yes, I am a queen, and will be treated as such, but I will follow your plan. I trust your judgment as you have been trained by the great Sherygha. I do love you, great man, and I look forward to this new life. So stand King Shaman, husband to Queen Zharda, and father to prince Shamanul."

The man stood up, filled with more pride than any point in his life. From that moment he had a mission. He would have to ensure that this fast growing village market became the new beacon of civilization for the world. If it was as successful as he anticipated, it could become the framework for all regions of Choi.

He spent the rest of the day getting to know and playing with his son. He talked to his now wife about the days at the fast growing village market. When the green and pearl dragon arrived, carrying fresh food, they ate and told her about the plan of secret relocation. He told her of the invisibility charm of the Ormaques and that he could not introduce her into to area yet, but once he learned the nature of the Arfaet people who dwelled there he would. However, there was a small mountain only a few miles away and she could live there amongst the other dragons. As for the queen, being thought dead for years she would stay hidden as she raised his son. The dragon was excited and fully compliant with the plan. That next morning, after eating a large helping of food, they packed the precious metals that dragons ate, as it had drastically increased in value among the last species, and took to the sky. Being much larger than Shaman, Lypara grabbed Zharda in her front claws and the two sacks filled with stones in her back.

They looked at the cave that had been their salvation over the past few years. Shaman, pulling out a handful of herbs from a small pouch began digging a hole. He placed just a small morsel of the herbs in the hole and covered it. Then he repeated it five more times, spanning the mouth of the cave. The man lifted his arms, and brought water across the ground in a straight line. The he lifted the moving water above the entrance and made them into what seemed like spikes. He then forcefully brought down his arms and the water arrows penetrated the earth at the exact six scuffs he made prior. With the blink of an eye, the mountain entrance seemed to have been covered. It looked to Zharda and Lypara that there was no opening, and simply the side of an average mountain. Shaman explained that it was one of many charms used for invisibility by his people. Each element mixed with the herbs created a different effect. They were used in different ways as well. Being of the water element, he mixed it with the earth to create this illusion for anyone who stumbles upon the area. He would keep the cave sacred to his family, and using it later when they needed. The Ormaque glimmered into a wyvern and grabbed the basket that swathed his infant son. Then he nodded to the dragon as they took to the sky towards the village market that would eventually become the cloister of Zhivy.

****

"What?!," yelled young Hikune, his voice full of disbelief and excitement. "The queen had not died, but was actually saved by Shaman. AND you mean they got married and had a baby. AND you said that he moved her to Zhivy with their son Shamanul. Wow. That is such a crazy thing. How was that even possible? Wasn't Glaridth the head Hufore though? Oh wait, they only THINK that he is. Oh wow. Even then, humans had to do things in such secrecy to protect their loved ones. Did Sherygha know?" The young boy's mind was spinning with inquisition. He had already learned so much, and it seemed at each turn, he found out something new, even more spectacular than before. He realized he had interrupted the Dama, so he quieted; then decided to change the subject. "So how did the celebration end? Was it as grand an affair as they thought it would be?"

The older man looked in the distance then continued the history lesson. "Well my boy, it was definitely an occasion to remember. In fact, for this part Hikarge had to fill in the gaps of the pages by using his ancestors' memories. You see, there is a smaller part that I will tell first.

"When Shaman arrived, he realized he could not

place his wife and child in his very small living quarters. So he asked the help of two other Ormaques to increase the space, saying he needed it for entertaining the other races, and teaching the elders and settlers how to heal with herbs. When that was finished he went back to the cave he found for Lypara and retrieved his family. He took Zharda first, leaving the baby with the dragon. And that same evening he retrieved the baby, still being careful not to be seen. Once the two had a secret, two roomed living space behind his, he did a different spell that made the doorway seem of the same mud made wall as the rest of his home. Only he knew the entrance, and would keep it that way. He would have to keep her existence a secret, possibly forever. Then he used a separate spell of protection on top of the existing one of concealment. By using his and Lypara's blood, it would become a sound barrier to all else but them two.

Over the next three years, whenever he returned back to his home from his month to month visits with Sherygha, he would bring a large satchel of water from the lake. He would drink minimally of the water, for it was there for healing his wife. She always seemed to get slightly better, but never for long. So he continued the treatment for years, hoping one day the beautiful queen would walk again."

Hikothe stood still as a statue for a moment, eyes looking around. His hand slowly eased to his blade handle. He was in a state of unease. Hikune realized his sudden change of tone and reacted accordingly. He also stood still, slightly turned for a different vantage point. There was a soft breeze in the air. A bird sang from a tree and another responded in his tune. A leaf began making its descent towards the earth. The sun was resting in the sky, sending warm rays to the planet as it trekked to its daily peak. All was nice and beautiful. It was a day that could last forever and none could complain. However, it was false. The stretch was not as it should be. One side of the road was vibrant with nature, while the left side was still and stagnant. And it was a stillness that only came before an ambush or fight. Hikune, did not know what he was looking for, but yet, he still stood there, looking around, eyes sharp, hand on his small blade as well. Hikothe scanned the tree line. Nothing seemed out of order, but he did not become the Dama of the world by not knowing the difference. The man went into one of the pockets of his pants and flung three balls into the woods at about the same interval. The first one landed, and smoke erupted from it and filled the air. The second ball he sent in the opposite direction. When it cracked against the ground a rancid fog blasted out of it, spreading outwards also. He then threw a third ball in the middle of the space and it blew apart. The smoke and chemical mixed with the flames and created an inferno in the dimly lit forest. Suddenly a small group of warriors darted out of the trees, some already burning, some infuriated by the Dama's tactics. They came towards to two screaming and ready for battle.

Hikune did not wait for his grandfather's instructions. He reached into back pouch and pulled out a light, steel throwing knife. He pitched the blade accurately and swiftly, hitting one of the attackers in the neck. He pulled out two more and heaved them both to separate attackers, each hitting vital spots and instantly ending their life. He looked to the right and saw Hikothe pull out his blade to meet the leading warrior. He swung upwards, knocking the man's blade to the side. Then he did a complete circle and thrust his sword into the man's chest. Still moving, he pulled it out and cut across another man's neck that was unfortunate to be running right behind the leader.

Two more reached the Dama, circling around him, hoping he would give one the advantage. His eyes looked towards right and then left. It was one against two, but still not evenly matched. Hikothe threw his large sword into the man on the left. He followed right behind it. When he reached the man, right as he was falling to the ground, he pulled the sword up with a jerk and leapt towards the still remaining fighter of the duo. He took a step towards him, but the red headed man with brown eyes jumped back. The soldier, wearing the blue of the Cloister closest to Aimone gave Hikothe information on who ordered the attack of the Dama. He saw the mark on the man's chest plate and hands, and also knew that these were not some ordinary soldiers. They were a specialist group, sent to assassinate the Dama and the future heir.

Infuriated by the presumption on his and his grandson's life, the large man pulled out the second sword he acquired the day before. He took two swift steps to the assassin and spun left. He brought both swords down to right in unison. Then he swung the right blade low and followed high with the left. The high blade hit the man in the head while he was dodging the lower. He stumbled backwards, holding his bruised head. Hikothe acted quickly, putting both blades to a cross and bringing them together with one swift motion. The body of the man fell while his head lobbed to the right, his hair now more red from blood than his nature.

Hikune saw his grandfather behead the soldier. Then suddenly another combatant was directly behind the Dama and would be able to kill him before he had time to react. He took another knife and sent it straight into the back of the assailant's head, sending him face first into the blood stained trail. He was turning around when a fisted hand, hidden behind metal gloves, reached his young face, knocking him to the ground. The man was menacing. He had heavy labored breathes from running, and the fresh red wounds of being unlucky enough to have been burnt by the acid fire. He reached down and grabbed Hikune by his hair. Then lifted him off the ground, barely able to speak he mumbled to the young dragon tender, "We will destroy the house of Hikothe. Then rule Aimone and bask in its many riches. He shall be the new Dam...." He was cut silent. The brown haired man looked down and saw a blade, driven into his chest, being held by a small hand.

"I will not die so easily," answered Hikune. "I am a future dragon rider, and descendent of Zharda the queen. Like my grandfather before me, I am smarter than you, barbarian." With that, the boy kicked the man in his crotch and was instantly released. He stood there, looming over there the dying man. Hikune retrieved his sword and cut off the man's head. Then he ran over to the last two men, still burning and unknowing of what was going on around them. He raised his blood stained blade high, grabbed it with both hands, and brought it down on one of the men, writhing in pain. It pierced through the burning back, severing his spine.

Hikune pulled his sword out and was going to kill the other attacker as well when his grandfather grabbed his hand. "No, my son," Hikothe yelled. "He is unable to attack us. We do not kill those who are defenseless. Once you kill a person, their face and memory stays with you. That is why we say "taking a life', because you take them wherever you go. Believe me this, leave a life when you can, or it will be a dark and painful road you will travel in your lifespan." The older man turned to the downed man, still crying from the scorching pain. He spoke to him sternly and without remorse, "I have spared your life. Do not forget this. Next time I see your singed face, I will drive my blade through it personally. Tell your Dama Regent, as well as the Dama himself, that his nerves are higher than his might. And also convey for me, that this day, after all these years, he is my enemy." Dama Hikothe knelt on the ground next to the only living attacker and took out a blade with his dragon rider emblem set in the gold handle. He grabbed the man's hand, burnt and tender, and stabbed the palm. He turned it left and right, digging a hole in his flesh that would never heal over properly. The man was screaming in agony while the old man worked. He took a handful of the bloodied dirt and pressed it against the open wound. Then he took a small, sharp pebble and used it to scrape away most of the soil he put in the wound. Hikothe reached into his pocket and pulled out a cloth strip. He placed the pebble inside the hand then wrapped it tightly with the fabric. He then repeated the same process with the other hand.

He hoisted himself and began gathering his things while his grandson still stood there, anger formed on his brow. He then spoke, "I have placed those pebbles in your hands for two reasons. The first is a reminder of your attack against our lives. The second is so as long as you breathe, your hands will never be able to wield a weapon without feeling the agony of the sharp stone under your skin." Then to Hikune, "go and gather your belongings as I have done. We are not finished our trek." The man then migrated to the middle of the now crimson road and began walking towards his destination again, humming to himself as if nothing had happened. However, Hikune now knew the tune and from it, his grandfather's mood. *Back to the Mother Tree They Go.*

A CHANCE MEETING

As the two walked, silence filled the space. Both were thinking personally, opposed to sharing their thoughts with each other. After some time Hikune softly chimed in on the now muted journey. "Can we continue grandfather? I would like to know how the houman race rose and fell. Also, how we survived everything. You said time has now balanced back out between the stories. It is two weeks before the celebration and Shaman just showed Glaridth the true power of the Ormaques. Please sir, continue."

Hikothe sighed, still feeling weary from the attack on his life by the neighboring Dama. He saw a small creek and decided to rest. He needed to eat and finally clean his weapons. When they reached the peaceful green water, he began speaking. "Hikune, did you collect all of the knives you threw from the dead bodies?"

"Yes," Hikune answered. "I made sure not to leave a single one. I even retrieved your dagger that you left."

Hikothe took the dagger from his grandson and placed it in the water with his two other blades. "Well like I said before. I had to go back to fill in the time between the stories as the world was swiftly changing in those years. Now time is the same again. It was two weeks before festival and word was spreading rapidly. Dragons that came and departed told other dragons they crossed paths with. Travelers would tell other villages or passerby caravans about the upcoming feast. It was the first cloister of the world. It signified the beginning of one single race of man. All who heard reveled in the joy and decision of the Zhivy council. The oldest species and the youngest would finally have one name to call the collective races, ***houman***.

"Zhivy was a cacophony of life and movement. Everybody was active. The citizens who lived there already were tidying their homes for the guests. The merchants were selling with more vigor so they had more to buy and barter with when more people arrived. The villages of the races that made up the cloister grew in the first week. Houmans were staying longer than the three day average. It was the busiest anyone, houman or dragon, had ever seen an area on earth.

As the day approached a large Black dragon flew overhead. He was followed by a black dragoness, and four smaller dragons. They circled the cloister of Zhivy, looking down at the progress. As they entered a fourth loop, a grey wyvern flew upwards to greet his company. "Great master Sherygha, I see you have brought your family as I asked. Please follow me to the lodgings I had built specifically for your size and family."

Shaman landed a few yards behind his own hut. Then he brought three other Ormaques to greet their leader. They were thrilled to see the dragon that protected and taught them since birth. The four Ormaques then stood in a square formation with their hands raised above them, showing their palms to the sky. First, one created a ball of air, the second swirled dirt around his body, peaking at his palm and then descending down and repeating. The third, a woman, shifted fire between her two palms, as almost a wave, and Shaman formed a mass of water. The four then moved their elements to the space between them. Earth mixed with water and made a long thick slab of mud. Then the fire engulfed it, turning it hard, almost like stone. Then the air caressed the object, smoothing its rough edges until a long pole stood before the audience of houmans and dragons. Shaman then took more water, and wetted the soil until the pole sank a third of its size. The four houmans then grabbed the pole and turned it counterclockwise for 180 degrees. As they reached the end, a large wind blew, and the trees that were there fell sideways, letting a large opening appear. The strong Ormaque had done it again. He and his kinsmen had created a large cave from the land with their power, and then masked it so none except the group here would ever know if its existence.

Shaman bowed to the dragons and spoke, "If it satisfies you Sherygha, please use this cave as home while you stay for the festivities. I have made it very spacious, as you, and your children are of the largest dragons I have ever seen. There are also small sections if any of you desire privacy while you sleep. I also set a room aside for me and my family, as I prefer to reside with you while you are here. In the back and above the smaller room for your stone hoard, is a chute for your waste to enter directly into the river. I have taken every precaution, and hope it is befitting such a regal dragon."

Sherygha, happy with the gesture from his friend laughed. "Of course I am thrilled Shaman. We will truly enjoy staying here with your family. I look forward to meeting the queen of once Hufore. I also want my children to meet her. We will enjoy these leisurely days with you old friend. I will like to learn much from this place. You report once a month to me, but it is not the same as experiencing it for myself. Is there anything else you wish to share before I rest?"

Shaman whistled and Lypara stepped forward from one of the smaller rooms in the back. She would be staying there as well. Normally Zharda would be riding her as not to be left on the ground for such an occasion. But it was not the case. As Lypara paced to reach to opening, Queen Zharda walked beside her. The other three Ormaques immediately knelt. Shaman was shocked to stillness. It was as if a dream of a dream had in fact been made into reality. The treatments of his Mageek water worked. Then he remembered that the last two times he gave her a tonic. Primarily of Mageek water, he also used a ground powder of dragon scales from all six types of dragon, the blood of a dragon, and special herbs with healing properties. With just two weeks of drinking the elixir, the queen had regained her ability to walk by her own will. It was indeed a joyous moment. She was ethereal, having the most regal of walks and air of nobility.

All the dragons walked inside. They met and mingled while eating three large fish and deer. The houman Vora had been brought along with the children as well. She enjoyed the company of the Sherygha clan. She also remembered the Ormaques that left the land of Mageek years ago and visited. They all sat in merriment and talked into the night. Later in the evening the other three purple eyed members returned to their homes, and Shaman closed the cloak once again, hiding the sight and sounds of the giant cave.

That night, as the three offspring of the two black dragons talked to Lypara at the back of the cave, Shaman, Zharda, Sherygha and Ellydra spoke on all subjects of life, mainly the growth of the families and the rapid growth of Zhivy over the past years. Put to work babysitting Shamanul, Vora was kept away so she could not hear the conversation. Then when all were tired, they slept

In the morning, the four younger dragons took to the sky as Lypara showed them the area from above. The two parental black dragons met with the elders of the villages and congratulated them on achieving such a milestone in their species' history. It seemed to the old dragon that even the Arfaet of Zhivy were not as blood thirsty as the multitude of their race. They did, however still keep the custom of wearing and selling dragon scales and parts. He decided that he would not chastise them right now, as everybody was jubilant over the fast approaching party, though the fact that there was a multitude of selling meant a multitude of dragon slaying, and he would have to figure out a way to remedy the now status quo.

The remainder of the week progressed rather quickly. Many more dragons arrived. Some Sherygha had not seen since they emanated through the arch so many years ago. One of such was named Duvotch. He was one of few, actually larger in size than Sherygha. However, he was much slower. Where Sherygha was majestic, broad and muscular, Duvotch was lazy and fat. He had minimal muscle density, and his neck was squat and thick. His belly was bloated, almost reaching the ground when on all fours. His claws were not sharp and his teeth were dull from over usage of eating. The enormous dragon would often eat an area dry of food, both of meat and vegetation. And once he devoured the habitat he would move on. That continued for centuries until Rynesch ordered him to live by the sea and eat from the multitude of fish and edible water based plants it can easily replenish. He was an ice dragon, thus one of the largest of the species. He was a white dragon with ruby edges. If he had not let himself get lazy, he would be a decent looking dragon. The High God made him, like the others from the timeless land. Duvotch was the only dragon to have two separate colors for his secondary colors. All of his edges were a ruby color, but right at the fine base of many of his scales was an amethyst tint. It made him look more dazzling than the other male dragons, and he knew it. Where he lacked strength, he made up in natural beauty. He often lofted around, only doing physical activity when he needed food. He was not a ferocious dragon, like many others, but could be very cruel in his own way. Some dragons had the ability to glamour others species into doing what they asked. Duvotch was one of them. His eyes sparkled and spun, and the beauty of his body would enthrall many of the lesser species. This was how he evaded enemies for centuries. Unfortunately, it was also how he collected houmans and animals as pets, slaves, and food at times. He was not a great dragon, but he spoke his mind, when serious, and in actuality was nicer than most.

"Duvotch, I have not seen much of you since we crossed the arch from the heavens, though I have heard much about you from other dragons. How are things faring for you?"

Duvotch looked at the smaller dragon and laughed. He spoke in his still raspy voice, "I see you have not gotten bigger Sherygha, though I see your muscle is even tighter than before. Oh my, oh my," he said loftily, "you must still strike fear in all dragons." Duvotch began turning as he spotted prey nearby. Then he inclined his fat head back and added "At least, to the ones who will actually still listen to you."

Sherygha cocked his head and held back a deep guttural growl, "Is that so. All dragons of this world will listen to me when I speak. If they do not, then I shall eat their hearts. Do you play coy with me, white dragon?"

Duvotch laughed and began lifting himself to the sky, wings straining from the stressful weight. Then he turned his massively horned head back and yelled to the black dragon, "I do as I please old friend. I do not hold your decree in esteem any longer. I see another dragon flying around, sporting the same color and edges as your most precious combination the High God gave you. He is young as well. I assume he is from your clutch. It would be a wise decision to tend to your children instead of provoking a larger dragon like myself." Then he turned his head to the sky as he made the slow ascent.

Sherygha, never one to be spoken down to immediately launched higher into the air. Being stronger had its privileges. He caught up to the fat dragon in a matter of seconds. Then he advanced past him, turned and retorted, voice deep and full of ire "You dare threaten me Duvotch. I have never troubled you, and yet on this day, you somehow find yourself superior to me. Do not forget that it was I the High God put as proctor over this planet. And if you dare try my patience again, I will rip those ruby red scales from your body and scatter them across the sea."

The lofty dragon did a light dip, laughing lightly. He looked to his left then responded, "Oh my, my. There they are. I see my own children have an escort. It would be troublesome of me to have my kids kill you. Not that they could anyway. But their escort is even larger than me, even if she is not of ice. My mate is quite strong as well. She also comes from the timeless land. Now, if *I* were to tell her to devour you, she would try. I don't know if she could, being that you are the strongest dragon, or simply claim to be, but I do know that she could cause immense pain that you would never forget, Black dragon." Then Duvotch darkened his voice and demeanor, "So if I were you I would recant my statement before I have my mate destroy you."

Sherygha looked at the arriving party. There was a white dragon with sapphire tint, fresh of wings, and barely keeping up. Another young white dragon, a female with amethyst edging, and a silver male with bright ruby tint were just ahead of the slower male. Then from behind her children a large dragon, largest he had ever seen appeared. She flapped enormous wings and he knew immediately who it was. She had left him confused over seven years ago. Now she returned with a mate and a clutch of her own. It was the silver and sapphire sky queen, Rynesch.

"Hello Sherygha. I see you have met up with my life mate already. I know it has been quite some time since you two have seen each other," she said while approaching with her usual grace. "I hope he has not been antagonizing you too much. I know he is jealous of you," she said with a chuckle. At the final statement of her oncoming the hefty white dragon growled softly. Apparently, Rynesch had compared the two dragons before.

"We have talked, yes. He was just telling me about his mate. I did not know he was referring to you. The callousness of his threats angered me, but for your sake, I will subside on his threats, at least this time. I will not be so generous in the future. It was wonderful seeing you again old friend. I look forward to catching up with you as the next few days come and go." Sherygha looked squarely at Duvotch and spoke, not hiding his words from the now gathered family, "I will kill you harshly if you dare threaten my life or my children again. Do not cower behind the Sky Queen, because if you have the audacity to tempt me again, it will be your last breath." Sherygha began to fly off, while his anger simmered. He was not a far distance and did a quick pivot in the air. He flapped his massive wings hard and made his body flat, accelerating through the air at high speeds. He swooshed past the three dragon children and rammed the considerably large pointed horns of his crest into the right side of antagonistic dragon. The white and dual tinted Duvotch roared in agony. His side colored a darker red than his edges. His scales covered the ground as he twirled into the landscape. Infuriated by the attack, he sent a long thick shard of ice to his former friend. Sherygha breathed a fire cloud at the projectile, melting and even evaporating it before it could do any damage to him.

All dragons knew that their levels of strength in their power varied. Some dragons could be physically obscure and have fire or water enough to destroy mountains. Other dragons could be as strong as a fortified boulder, but not have enough power to even kill a grown houman. They could in fact train and develop their gifts, just like any other, but many did not. As they grew, they simply accepted how potent their elemental power was and continued their life. Thus, when Duvotch attacked Sherygha, it was a mere response, not to be taken seriously by the strongest dragon on earth.

"Why have you attacked my mate captain Sherygha?" asked Rynesch.

"Your fat, lowly mate threatened to attack me and my children. He also told me I have no jurisdiction over him now that he has been mated to you. I simply reminded him that I am the strongest of us all. And there was no amount of glamour he could use, or beauty he could flaunt that would ever change that. I do apologize to your highness for my brutish behavior, but some things are necessary. I will be returning to Zhivy to feast with my family. I truly hope you will stop by to meet my mate and clutch."

"My captain, I am sorry for how crude my mate behaved. I believe I dote on you too much and after all these years, he has developed resentment to you. As for your meal invitation, I and my clutch would love to join you. I look forward to meeting your children. Though I am unsure about Duvotch's joining us."

"My mate," responded Sherygha, "will be there as well. She will be thrilled to finally meet you."

Looking away she answered, "Yes, but of course. I shall see her there as well."

Sherygha took to the sky again. He did not look back at the injured dragon. He did notice however, that neither of his family aided him either. The large black dragon took a small bit of delight in that fact. They flew across the cloister center and landed near the water. Awaiting him was his mate, children, and their new friend, the dragon, Lypara.

"This is my oldest and clutch winner, Sherybi. Of all four of my heirs he is the only one with my exact coloring, the second ever in existence. He is even an ice user like me. Next is my red lightning princess, Shedrya. As you see, she is my only child not to wear black scales. Then are my twins, bearing the colors of their mother, Ryghari of earth, and Ellygha of Fire. They are all strong like me. They are even larger than most other dragons of equal age, and wiser. I am truly proud of them. And this, my dear friend is the fire goddess Ellydra. She is my mate for life, and mother of my clutch."

Rynesch looked at the large dragons. They were marvelous. She almost cried for the fourth time in her life. She could not help but let the nagging thought cross her mind, 'these should be our children my dear and wonderful dragon'. She greeted each dragon child, then was told about Lypara and greeted her as well. She settled across from Sherygha and introduced her three dragons. "This, my old friend is the strongest and winner of my clutch, Jysmun. She is the element water. Second is Rynatch. He uses ice like you…' then Rynesch quickly added, 'and his father." She then continued at her original pace. "Thirdly is my earth expending son, Fyndesch. Looking at the young dragons, it seems they are all around the same age, like cousins; or even siblings." The largest dragon ever created or hatched then relaxed and fell to her knees. The others in the party followed and they all feasted on the large meal prepared by Shaman and the Ormaques.

Later that night, when the other dragons left, and her offspring out rough housing with the sky queens kids, Ellydra approached a resting Sherygha. "That horror of a queen! How dare she not acknowledge me? I was so looking forward to meeting her and then she acted as if I were not there. Like I was a small insignificant illusion that the houmans have when they dehydrate. I know I cannot attack her, but I would like to understand why she spent the entire day in our company, eating the food brought for us, and only speaking to me when I ask her a direct question. And how many times did she refer to the young dragons and siblings between the two of you. I AM YOUR MATE! She should be lucky I am not from the bright land with no time like my grandparents or yourself, or I would have certainly attacked her!" Rage festered within Ellydra. She began breathing fire at the walls and once at the metals below. A curious thing happened; the metals began to melt and eventually formed a jagged ball, beautiful with colors.

Shaman asked if he could examine it but was refused. The dragoness was in no mood to appease anyone. She jumped over, growled at the powerful Ormaque and ate the rough sphere of collected metals and stones. She continued on her rant, "How can she sit there, smug and high, while her mate gorges himself like a pregnant sow. I was surprised when he approached us. He was larger than even you, but was fat and lazy. Why would the Queen of Dragons settle and mate with such a horrible choice. Now, I see he has corrupted her into becoming a dragon of horrible character. I am truly disappointed."

Sherygha finally stood and walked over to meet her. They move around so much that he sometimes forgets how much larger he is than she. He looked down at his mate and then pivoted on one foot. He brought his long strong tail around and struck the much smaller black dragon across the side. He then snarled at her and pushed her against a wall. "Do not ever speak ill of the Sky Queen in my presence! She was the High God's very first creation. She was made thirty one dragons before myself by the creator. She has been my general in the two battles for the timeless land, as well as the head dragon here on earth. She personally selected me to be her only captain to govern this world. We have been friends for thousands of years, and shall remain friends for thousands more." Sherygha turned away and began walking to the exit. While walking he continued, "She has seen many dragons mated. Also seen many killed. And I am now positive that she expected me to be her dance champion and clutch mate. Though, at the time I did not know."

"Why didn't you then, black dragon. Why did you not fly off and overpower her with your great strength. Then give her all the many clutches she has obviously been waiting to lay? Tell me dragon, tell me now!" shrieked an agitated Ellydra.

Sherygha looked outside to ensure privacy, and then lifted the veil of seclusion made by Shaman. Right before he exited he answered the crying dragon, "When she came to me, I told her of a dragoness I could not find after learning her name. I did not understand why she acted so strangely until this day. I was blinded you see. Only focused on finding that sole black and silver dragon I wished to dance with forever. Think about that." He then walked out, and closed the protected cabin. He looked up at the sky and sniffed. After a few whiffs, he found what he wanted and flew in that direction.

Just past the village of the Norfex, a large crowd, filled with what seemed like all the citizens and visitors of Zhivy was watching a large group of young dragons doing battle in the distance on the open plain. Even a few older dragons that came for the celebration watched their species with pleasure. This type of rough housing was a dragons' nature while young. It taught them how to hone their skills all while showing dominance. It pleased Sherygha to see his four dominating the large group of power filled creatures. He counted twenty dragons, give or take one or two being hidden in the fray. They all varied in size and color, getting their unique features and colors from their parents and grandparents. He saw his offspring winning battles, two even three at a time. Even Shedrya, unable to truly fly, was using her lightning to constrict and cripple her opponents and her lithe elegant frame to outmaneuver others. There, through the battle royale, was the enormous Rynesch. She was there alone, watching her three children win some bouts and lose others. He leapt into the air, flying high above the raucous to avoid being hit by an open flying blast of power that missed its intended opponent. Especially from his own four powerful children. He landed next to Rynesch and continued watching the event, on the eve of the HOUMAN celebration, as it was being called.

"You have upset my mate," began Sherygha. "She idolized you. She wanted to meet you more than anything else these past few years. Then she does, proud to show you her clutch, and you say no more than eight words to her. That is not the behavior I would expect from you my highness."

Rynesch pondered a moment, still watching Sherygha's brood thrash any dragon that attacked them, including her own slightly smaller clutch. Then she spoke softly, "there was a time dear dragon, that I would have scolded you for using such pleasantries while we speak privately. Now I like them. I think it will do some good for you to use them and remember your place when speaking to me. To speak plainly, I care not of your mate." She paused, letting her anger and embarrassment subside, then continued, "Jealousy is in a dragon's nature, some more than others. However I do not envy any of this world… except *her.* She is youthful, wise for a dragoness of the younger generations, and moves so much more graceful than I ever have. I can easily see why you became infatuated with her, though in truth, I hate that you did. Nevertheless, I will apologize tomorrow before the festival while we eat the morning meal. She cannot help what she does to my emotions, but I can however, control how I act towards her." She finally looked at the majestic black dragon. Then she scratched him along the neck, drawing a small drop of blood. She drank the dragon's blood and mind spoke with him so only he could hear. "I am truly sorry I offended her Sherygha. I am also sorry that my mate decided to cause conflict with you. Our houses will not be at war while I live…" She then desperately added, "Please tell me she makes you happy. If not, I will leave them, my clutch, my lazy mate, all I have, and I will fly away with you right now to any corner of the world the High God made for us. I am the sky queen, but will be your servant and caretaker for the rest of eternity. Speak it Sherygha and I will be wholly yours, dear dragon."

Sherygha sat silent. He understood her thoughts, but never realized they were for him. It was a stark reality hearing the beautiful silver and sapphire dragon confessing her love to him. If she had done it sooner, he would have been more than happy to take her as a mate. As he sat there, he realized he in fact had wished it from her at one point in time. She was strong and wise. Her scales were perfectly shaped. The sapphire edges accented beautifully against her silver coloring. The High God made her in the image of his great castle. She was a magnificent dragon of great wisdom. Why hadn't he realized it sooner? He turned and met his evening companion face to face, staring at her deep green eyes. Why is this the first time he realized that, he thought? Then he mind spoke to her "The houmans have an act they call kissing. It offers affection at times, and lust at others. However, they only do it when they are enthralled by the person they find pleasing. If we were houman, right now I would kiss you, beautiful Sky Queen." He turned back to the brawl, but moved closer so still they could only hear each other. "You told me to not give you such formality. Nevertheless I always do. It's not so I know my place, but that I show you how much I respect yours. I cannot and will not leave my family. My mate has never let me down. She was all I wanted and more. My hearts belong to her, forever." He then turned away and opened his wings, readying himself to take flight. "Alas, there is a small corner of my heart that still swells and beats a bit faster when I am around you. I believe the heart is like pillars or columns. There is a pillar for each person I love. Some are higher than others. So even though your pillar is not the highest or largest, it is indeed large, as well as the oldest and most rooted. Please remember, even though I am happy and will not abandon my family, I do love you, my Sky Queen. I'm sorry I could not be your mate. But I will always be a very 'fond' friend." Sherygha lightly bit Rynesch's tail, lingering longer than either of them expected, and then took to the sky, returning to his mate.

The next morning, while the sun was still rising, Rynesch, Sherygha, and Ellydra went out for a hunt.

They found it difficult at first with three dragons. Yet, as time progressed they quickly worked out a system of using the massive dragons to scare out prey in a cattycorner direction. With only one direction to flee, the smaller dragon, Ellydra would attack and swiftly take down the meal. They each ate a fresh kill. Then each carried one back for the other dragons. The children should have been fending for themselves but the parents knew that in all truth, they were still barbing each other with words and hitting each other with their power in a massive amount of play. It was rare to see more than five youthful dragons in one space for long periods of time. It pleased the elder dragons, so in return they hunted for their young as well.

After breakfast, the day went off with splendid festivity. The first major celebration in houman history was spectacular. Multiple vendors of each race set up small tents to sell their food, equipment, or trade. Smoked meats with sweet red and green sauces were served by the Uckleet. They also marketed their trademark dragon scaled armor and weapons. They also offered service to excavate a cave for expecting dragons or houmans who preferred the stone walls. Many beards, adorned with jewels could be seen. Mountain moving and merchants were the two primary characteristics of the Uckleet. Under King Dwarfe, the Uckleet and their founding families grew to new riches. Mining out the jewels and precious stones that the dragons ate had seen true profits. For as the dragons desired them, houmans did even more. The stones, ruby, sapphire, amethyst emerald, and onyx were always in high demand. However, demanded even more than stones were the metals, copper, silver and gold. The colored stones and the metals was where a dragon originally got its edging from. All dragons were created by the same elements the High God used for the world. Many were of the stone colors, but a select few, generally the strongest and chosen of the high god were blessed with copper, silver or gold edges. Eating the stone color that you wore, would give your scales strength and vitality. However, if you ate the more precious silver or gold, everything strengthened. Not just your scales, but also your senses, muscles, and claws. Thus, where the Uckleet were working, there was always a dragon or two around, vying and bartering for the stones they unearthed.

The space between the rows of tents was wide, allowing the attending dragons to roam between them with the houmans. As the Uckleet were peddling their ores, the Ormaques were offering to the crowd a precious item, unable to get anywhere else; something they called pearls. It was a rare coloring for dragons of pearl edges. They often times could not eat enough metals to sustain their scale luster. Thus, the Ormaques all sold them to the highest of bidders. Dragons desired them, causing the houmans to desire them even more. Alongside the pearls, the grey race sold exotic fresh and smoked meats and aquatic vegetation and herbs. Being the most exclusive of the races, many people went to their tents just to glimpse them live. Scattered throughout the center cloister were Mageek tents. The few daring Ormaques would show the power of Mageek. They knew better than to show their full power, but they did small tricks with their element, or playing off their comrades' power to make an illusion. All who witnessed the show marveled over the spectacle. Many left the display in awe and would return or visit another. Word spread through the crowd that these tents were showing 'magic'. The grey people inside could do beautiful 'magic' and it was nothing short of spectacular. They could call birds out of thin air or move fire and water with their hands. It was even said, that they could make a person disappear and reappear in the crowd. Other tents showed exotic animals never before seen. They presented large abnormal wolves or birds with legs of a reptile, and bodies of a beast. There were fish with hands instead of fins and apelike beasts with wings. All present at the festival heard of the magic Ormaque tents, and since then, the word has never changed. All things that seemed supernatural, whether real or an illusion was forever deemed to be the magic of the Ormaques.

Many Mylare tents offered the berries of the forest they resided in. One in particular was a fist sized green and blue berry called an elf berry. It had dazzling effects after eating it. The chemicals of the fruit would cause heightened senses and physical traits. The hunters would eat one before leaving to bring back a large game animal. However, when overindulged it could cause a houman, and even a smaller dragon to enter a hypnotic state. They would think they were flying while sitting down. They would laugh at random moments and then anger right after. It was of the most pleasurable feelings a houman could have, more so than drinking the strong ale of the Hufore or Uckleet. Thus, it became the most profitable item the Mylare could sell. It had highly addictive attributes and many returned over the next three days to purchase them from who they called elf people.

The Norfex did not have a grand amount of goods to sell. However, they did have two things that changed the history of mankind. Like the elf fruit had often times changed the name of the Mylare, or the new magic of the world, the food called bread, baked rolls of wheat, and honey, the excretion they took from a hoard of flying insects they called bees, took this new world by storm. In small pockets, the Norfex had shown their bread and honey to some villages they passed through, but now, here at the HOUMAN celebration, all of the elders of the world could taste the richness of the cooked wheat and the sweet secretion of bees. They also made a type of ale based of honey and wheat called mead. It suited the lively race as it enhanced their spirits.

Everywhere in the cloister people were moving. It was vibrant and loud. It was a great feeling for the Arfaet merchants that were participating. The arfaet tents sold many forms of weapons and shields. They also sold their services as escorts and mercenaries, but would not offer their infamous dragon hunting. In actuality, most of the arfaet did not hunt dragons like most of the people believed. In truth, though they almost all feared and disliked them, most would not dare cross one. The story of their beginning was told mandatorily by the village elder to all eleven year old children. They were told of their history and on how the eleventh hour of life, the dragon attacked them and the women helped heal them. Now, true to their heritage, the race was filled with subservient women and barbaric warriors. Many Uckleet hired them as escorts for their merchant trips. Today was no different. Even the Norfex sponsored many from these tents for the upcoming voyages home after the three day event.

Lastly, the Hufore were scattered throughout the cloister. Some tents sold the meat and herbs they were known for eating. Others sold the pottery of burnt mud and tight water sacks to the new people. However, many tents, staying true to their beliefs, offered workshops of knowledge. The participants would learn how to make the dishes from mud. They showed them how to build faster, stronger structures. There were classes on fire and water usages. A few tents even taught agriculture. However, one pavilion, large and open, showed how to properly identify and care for a dragon. Various Hufore worked the grand display. There was one however, a young beautiful Arfaet woman who seemed more knowledgeable than the rest. It was Vora.

Now a young woman, and advocate against the hunting of dragons by her people, blonde haired Vora stationed the dragon exhibit. She spoke on how the dragons gained their coloring. How the sizes varied between a single clutch due to lineage and power element. She showed the crowds how eating the rocks and metals dug up by Uckleet effected the scales and claws of dragon. She knew the parts of a dragon, inside and out. And most of all, after spending years tending dragons, she knew how they thought. Taught mostly by Sherygha, the houman Vora understood more about dragons then even some dragons. She insisted on doing the workshop, even when Shaman and Zharda thought against it. Vora suggested to the duo, that if more people connected with dragons, knew their history and how they came to be, how they operated and thought, then they would fear them less, and eventually the two dominant species on the planet could thrive together.

It was on the third day, when the old dragon Sherygha decided to be the dragon that stood for the houman to use. She asked him questions and he answered truthfully. It was the largest crowd she had of the days there. When people heard that the proctor of the world was being used for the demonstration, they flocked in droves to see. Due to his large size, the onlookers did not even need to be close. Vendors closed temporarily, citizens left their homes, and people of the village migrated. The entire carnival seemed to come to a halt as almost everybody came to watch.

"Great dragon father, why do some dragons attack us, while others do not? Were you not placed here to guide us by the High God?" asked Vora to her assistant.

"It was not as you think. You must understand, we dragons were offered this paradise from the High God. He gave it to us for thousands of years before he ever mentioned creating your species to live alongside us." Then he reluctantly added, "He did ask us, however, to help you mature and prosper as a species. The difficult truth is, once we crossed through the celestial arc to gain our elemental power, we also gained free will, like you houmans." Sherygha looked around, as his demanding voice had everyone's attention, houmans and dragons alike. So he continued, "Many dragons are thousands of years old, as it takes us nearly a decade to produce and raise young. We are an old species; older than your animals and even your dinosaurs. We were here when he created the Norfex, first of the houmans. We are still here now, as you have begun the journey to completing the High God's will and cross mating until you are one sole species. Dragons are here to help you, if you let us. However, hunting my brethren will only incite others into retaliation."

The crowd applauded at the sincerity and truth to the dragon's answer. Vora continued, changing to subject to keep the people fresh and listening, "So I know that a color of a dragon can change, and the edges worn are based from the jewels and metals of the earth, as planned by the high God. However, in all my years, I have never seen another black dragon with gold edging except your son. Why is that, my lord of skies?"

Sherygha was stunned. It was not a difficult question, but one he had not thought about for thousands of years. The grand dragon let out a soft laugh as he saw Rynesch staring at him, awaiting his answer. "I, my little friends, was created by the High God himself. I was the forty second creature to ever breathe life. Each of us first fifty dragons had something unique upon creation. The Sky Queen, first creation of the High God was colored after his palace, silver and sapphire. Others mimicked different things. I am black, stemming from his powerful sword. His handle is made of pure gold. Thus, when he created my egg, he took the black ore from the blade and the pure gold from the handle and wove it into my being. My colors are of royalty and power. He forged his blade himself right before the first war of the timeless land. Thus, I was created with the same things and purpose. That is why no other dragon until my first born son is black of scale and touched with gold like myself. That is also why I am the captain to the sky queen and absolute governor of this world. I was created to wield immense power." He felt the pride that memory. It had been such a long time since he reminisced about it. Yet, more than that, he remembered his time with his creator.

"If you could count back, exactly how old are you?" asked the smiling Vora.

"Well it is impossible to tell you. In the timeless land, we did not keep track of things like that. My nature is to be eternal. Which is why, unless killed, I will not die on this planet either. However, if I take the rate at which our wings grow and …" Crash! A loud blast came from the crowd. People scattered and screamed frantically with all their strength. Sherygha looked at the disturbance but saw only a large ball of shattering ice. Then above him the even larger dragon Duvotch roared loud and strong. He dropped down on the displayed dragon, pinning his wings and arms to the ground. He scratched at the dragon's exposed wing joints and bit into his back. Sherygha turned on his side and whipped his tail across Duvotch's face, making sure his tail horns hit first. The ice dragon stuttered backwards, trying to regain his composure. The black dragon swiftly scrambled to his feet, trying not to allow his enemy any more chances to attack. When Sherygha began to do a dash towards the white opponent, a swift tail with small horns struck upwards at his open underbelly. He looked down as he moved away in pain. It was Rynatch, the ice user. White like his father with sapphire like his mother, he would have been just as beautiful as his parents and clutch siblings, but now all the large dragon saw was a young dragon, about to be void of life.

Sherygha leapt on top of the small dragon. Youth had some advantages as the dragon nearly escaped. However the older dragon caught him by the tail as he was making a break for safety. Crunching down with massive jaws, he tore the tail apart while also pulling the body back. He grabbed the small dragon and began lifting him when a solid ball of ice struck him across his golden plated chest. Sherygha tumbled backwards, still holding the small dragon child. He righted himself and launched a stronger ice pallet back at Duvotch. It struck him in the side, knocking him to the ground. Rynatch reached across while being held and bit the enormous dragon on the arm, tearing off scale and flesh. Sherygha roared loud and agonizing. He took the dragon by the head and bit into its neck, just missing one of his hearts. The other, took a large tooth, deep into its bloody mass. He then threw the young dragon in the direction of his mother. But when he looked up, Rynesch was no longer there. She, along with Ellydra, was herding houmans away from the free for all battle that had suddenly erupted. Sherygha felt a sharp pain in his back as Duvotch had raked his claws in a deep swipe across his spine. He fronted to his arms and kicked the giant dragon with his hind legs. Sherygha, the strongest dragon on the planet was about to show the fat dragon his true strength. He faced the larger dragon. By only looking, it would seem an unfair fight. Duvotch outsized the black dragon by a couple of hundred pounds. He had more horns on his crest and spine. He even looked more menacing than the regal black and gold dragon. However, the looks were completely wrong. Where Duvotch was larger, he did not possess half the muscle as Sherygha. His horns were slightly more plentiful, but were not sharp like the better dragon, and as far as power goes, Sherygha was naturally stronger and possessed both, fire and ice. He looked like a fool facing the white opponent, but he knew that in just a few short moves, he could kill Rynesch's mate.

Sherygha breathed in a large amount of air and sent a blast of fire and ice to the opposite dragon. Duvotch attempted to move, but was too slow and took a hit against his right leg. He screamed but straightened out. He opened his gigantic wings and stood on his hind legs, showing the world how large in size he truly was. The viewers gasped in fear and awe as they watched this giant at full display. The only other dragon people had seen larger than Duvotch was the sky Queen herself. However, Sherygha was a veteran warrior. While standing, trumpeting to the world his massive size, Sherygha sent another blast of fire and ice to his chest. Duvotch, only just coming down, took the hit squarely against his ruby chest plate.

It sent him spiraling across the land. Sherygha then displayed his size to the world, reminding them that he was no meager dragon either. Then he landed and ran full speed to the rolling dragon. The screaming Jysmun landed just before him and begged him to stop. As a dragon, wise like her mother, she could see the obvious difference in power and skill level. She pleaded with the black dragon not to kill her father. Then, as Sherygha was just about to agree and leave to heal himself, Duvotch reached his daughter and growled at her. "You dare interfere with my bout, girl. Go with your mother and brother and assist the houmans. I do not require your assistance. Now leave before I kill you along with him." The white dragon then reached out with his claw and swiped his daughter across the jaw, sending her soaring across the span and into a group of watching houmans. He returned his attention to Sherygha, "Now for your demise, foolish dragon." Duvotch took to the air, heading towards his watching mate. Sherygha followed, pain jolting him with every beat of his wing. His joints ached from the attacks and the holes in his leather flaps made it hard to gain altitude or speed. Nevertheless, he followed his opponent. As he approached the dragon, it seemed Duvotch glimmered across his body. He then saw his eyes, swirling in a clockwise pattern. Suddenly he knew what had happened. He looked at Rynesch and saw her daze and shake her head as if trying to free an insect from her ear. She then looked at the landing Sherygha and stood even taller. She thundered and ran towards him, knocking down anyone and anything in her path. She covered half the distance when black and silver Ryghari landed in front of her, letting loose a large canvass of earth shards. The dazed dragon simply leapt over the small dragon like she was nothing more than a drakka still learning her element. Right above her she brought down her tail like a strong whip, lodging a horn into Ryghari's neck, and then ripping it away as she was still moving forward to Sherygha. The small dragon yelped and fell back. She shot earth pellets in response to the attack, but aiming it at none in particular. The siblings helped Ryghari to her feet and carried the young dragon to their mother.

"I do not wish to fight you Rynesch. You know I can overpower you old friend. Do not do this. It is glamour. He is using you to keep himself safe. Please listen to me, I am your friend," begged Sherygha.

"You are NOT my friend, old dragon. I will kill you for my mate. Then I shall feed your body to my children so they may grow large like yours." Rynesch sent out a torrent of wind. Sherygha jumped to the side to avoid it, but ended up closer to her as she changed direction. She rammed into his left side with her nose horn, tearing off a piece of his body as her momentum and large stature sent the smaller black dragon thundering into the ground. She jumped over to him and stomped on his chest. And then took her massive claw and brought it down on his unprotected stomach. Dust surrounded the land. In some places were fires. The spectators could no longer see the harsh battle, however when Sherygha received the large, excruciating wound, all within miles heard the roar.

Rynesch boomed to the blackening sky. She stood on her hind legs and opened her wings to capacity. The fearful audience could see her ostentatious silhouette through the smoke and dust. The largest dragon of creation was showing her full physique, and all that watched, including the dragons, succumbed to the truth of the sky queen's aptitude and potency. She was no mere dragon, but a force of nature, never to be perturbed. Rynesch looked down at Sherygha and raised her arms again as she prepared to open the blood filled crevices of his stomach completely and kill the dragon she loved. She heavily brought down her massive claws with intent to kill when unexpectedly she jolted. Shocked and confused she looked around at what could have happened. She then was hit by a ball of ice to her face and blast of fire to her back almost simultaneously. She turned and saw the other two of Sherygha's children standing there. As the realization hit her, so did another attack from the fire and ice dragons. She sucked in air. Rynesch would kill the children first and then quickly finish off their injured father. As she reached the peak of her growing power, she realized the red dragon was breathing in as well, but before she could release her storm on the trio, Shedrya loosed a thick, lightning fast attack on the oldest of dragons. It easily stunned her. Then, before she could regain her composure another bolt struck her. Again, before she could react, a third jolt shocked her large body. Shedrya kept sending bolts of lightning to cripple the sky queen, just like nature had done to her father some time before. At that point of being continuously struck by lightning, she became barraged by blasts of fire and ice all across the span of her gigantic body. The sheer speed and multitude of the attacks was relentless. Sherygha had taught them well. And why wasn't he attacking her? Surely he was healed enough by now, but he lay there, watching his children barrage her with their power.

The elemental battering hurt the dragon. Then as the nature of cause and effect would have it, fire melted the ice and turned into water. The water mixed with the lightning enhanced the shock to greater proportions. She was trapped in a state of stasis, being destroyed while unable to return the aggression. The old dragon Rynesch wholly knew what was happening, but could terminate the assault nonetheless.

Crippled and on her knees, she grabbed the earth for support. She would not be able to receive many more of the harsh attacks on her body for much longer...

Buzzzz… Rynesch felt as if she was frying. Her scales created a reverberation from the massive vibrating of the jolts. She opened one eye just enough to see the red dragon sending one more, large steady stream of lightning to her. The sky queen realized it was over. She was going to die. And worst of all, she would die to the children she wished were her own. Her actual children were keeping to themselves. Only one fought, and on the wrong side. Why, she wondered, did Rynatch attack Sherygha with his father after she told him to stay out of it? Now he was on the verge of death, and she would die directly before him. And for that matter, why had she also chosen to attack her captain? She had warned her mate and told him that she would not intercede if he continued on the path of jealousy and vengeance yet here she was… Glamour! She had allowed her mind to be glamourized by the beautiful dragon and spinning eyes. Such a fool she was, and now she would lose her life, while he ran off like the coward he was… Buzzzz. Rynesch closed her eyes and accepted her fate, unable to sustain her will to fight. Her want of a mate led her to Duvotch, and through Duvotch, her demise. Horrible, was pain she felt. It was unbearable. She let out a final soft sigh and coughed. She mind spoke one last time to the black dragon "I still love you my grand captain." Then her body collapsed to the ground.

Sherygha, slowly standing, watched his children work together to bring down the sky queen. He felt conflicted over her death, but clear on why she attacked him. He knew that had he wanted, he could have killed her. Not easily, but he would have emerged victorious. However, he couldn't, he absolutely could not be the one to take his oldest friend's life. Luckily his heirs saw his reluctance and stepped up to the challenge. "Children, leave the sky queen. You have protected me, but we are not finished. Shedrya, you have spent most of your power and cannot fly. Go with Lypara and take Ryghari to Shaman to be healed. Sherybi and Ellygha, you will come with me. First however, make a dome of earth and ice to cover the great dragon, and then I'll create a moat of fire for extra protection. I will not have greedy houmans hacking her body for profit. We will kill Duvotch. His power of glamour killed my oldest friend. Now we will return the favor." Sherygha had been healing himself while his kids attacked Rynesch. He was not in the best of circumstances, but his body would hold for one more battle.

The three dragons set out to the sky. Standing directly to the right of them, Duvotch was healing himself. The trio did not wait to attack. Taking orders from their father through a mind link, they again barraged the old dragon with blasts of fire and ice. Though this time, they did not hold back. There were no feelings of regret as they had felt when fighting with the silver and sapphire queen. They rained down the elements given to them from birth. The old dragon was being hit so much he could not fully retaliate. However, without their sister shocking him into a stupor, he still tried to avoid some, and even sent back a blast or two of ice. The two youthful dragons circled and spit power at the large white. He eventually tried to fly away. Sherybi was first to clasp his wing with his jaws. He held on, tearing his wing flap and biting apart his joints while ripping chunks out of his left leg and arm. His brother Ellygha reached him second but closer to the spinal ridge. He dug his sharp claws into the base joint, connected to his spine and severed it. Duvotch howled in pain as he fell back down to the surface, uneven and circling. His right wing came free from his body right before impact. His left wing, dislocated at various points and the flap torn to shreds would offer no help either. He was grounded, and in immense pain.

Sherygha reached the crashed dragon and laughed. Then he said plainly and loudly, "I am the strongest of all dragons. You thought to use my friend against me with your glamour. But, old dragon, that did not work. My children have been trained by me since the first day of hatching. I asked you to not bother me, but you could not appease your own desires. So now I will appease my own desires. I have not been as forthcoming about my power as you think. I can indeed use fire, but my true power comes from deep within the earth. And after all these thousands of years, I can finally use it." Sherygha stood tall as he could and breathed in a steady breath. Then out of his nose a frosted haze fell on the land in front of him. Slabs of ice covered the ground on two sides of the white dragon, creating an alley and joining at the tips, creating walls of ice. He breathed in, deep and guttural and grumbled. He trumpeted loudly, half screaming and half roaring, remembering his queen's final words. Sherygha opened his mouth and red boiling liquid oozed out between the two slabs of ice. It flowed swiftly down the created ice channel. Duvotch tried to move backwards to avoid the sweltering red mass but was too injured. As the lava kept steadily moving, Sherygha watched as another of the original fifty dragons began losing their life. The once beautiful dragon tried to reach out of the searing flood, screaming in complete agony. His scales were holding off some of the heat, but would only endure a short while. They soon, as all things do, would melt into the liquid fire and then the magma would cook his large body. Sherygha closed his mouth and blew another plate of ice at the entrance in front of his feet. The lava would pool only that spot, leaving the rest of the terrain intact. He looked at the now burning dragon, being slowly consumed by his truest power. While Duvotch shrieked and roared in agony he spoke to him one last time. "I told you before, Duvotch, I am the strongest of the land. I was created by the high God himself to ensure the survival of this planet. My true element is not simply fire, but lava itself. Now die slowly. Your ability to heal will keep trying to lengthen your life, but my lava will inevitably engulf you entirely. It will be a pain even your descendants shall not be able to assuage." Sherygha stood there with his two male heirs, watching the lava boil over the dragon. The screaming had finally subsided, but he was not fully dead yet. With a roar he lifted his head in defiance one last time, looking for any means of escape or help. He desolately realized there were none. Having no scales left, he steadily sank into the blistering pool of lava.

FILAR CROSSING

Hikune reached the cave entrance first, excitedly calling for the dragon Hikarge. The duet had been traveling all night after the incident, and the boy direly wanted to sit and rest, but would not divulge that to his never complaining grandfather. He yelled for the blue dragon once more when he heard the roar of another dragon. Thundering towards the entrance was a dragon that was not Hikarge. Showing a nose horn, the dragon must be female. She was white with an amethyst edge. She lifted her head and released a blast of water. Hikune jumped to the edge of the cave, plastering himself along the wall. When the second blast came, he rolled on the floor to his original position. Then, looking up he again moved to the left wall, avoiding a third attempt to injure him. He looked at the dragoness and spoke hastily, "Beautiful dragon queen, I mean you no harm. I am laying down my sword so you know that I would never bring harm to a creature such as marvelous as you." Hikune now knew that flattery pleased a dragon, and as he intended, the female dragon ceased attacking the young boy.

"Leave my grandson alone Sheffe," yelled Hikothe. "He is here with me to meet with Hikarge. Where is my grand dragon?" Then he added, "You look magnificent as always."

The white dragon chuckled. Then as she turned she spoke, "He is farther in the back eating a large horned beast. Your grandheir flatters even better than you old man. Follow me." Facing the inner quarters of the cave, Sheffe grabbed Hikune with her tail and brought him to her face. "I apologize, descendant of Hikothe. It is a pleasure to finally meet you. I shall carry you to rest of the way my little friend."

Hikune looked at her and smiled. He spoke hesitantly, "Are you a child of Rynesch and Duvotch? I believe your father was white and amethyst also correct?"

Sheffe kept her face forward as she walked, though she did in fact bristle when the name Duvotch was offered to the atmosphere. "My great grandsire was different. He was one of the original dragons created by the high God, though it seems you already know that." She then sent a look to the close following Hikothe. Then she continued, "He was actually the only dragon to have his edging one color, and his scale tint another. So his children took both colors. Duvotch was white with ruby edges. My grandmother was white with amethyst like myself. Her name was… "

"*JYSMUN*," Hikune excitedly cut in.

Laughing at the youth, she continued, not minding the intrusion, "yes dear one. My grandmother was Jysmun. She was beautiful. She bore my father, Pyla, silver and ruby."

They reached a fork in the path and went to the right even though Hikune was sure he heard sounds of water coming from the left. Soon after the veer they saw the blue dragon finishing off the animal, blood and bones splattered across the room. Hikarge looked at his new mate and his old friend. He let out a soft purr seeing his favorite people in the world at the same time. He was hatched by the old man, but just finished dancing with Sheffe only a year ago. She still had not laid eggs, but now being of the eternal year, he no longer put much emphasis on time. When she was ready, he would take her to the upper level, housing the egg shelf where they would raise his first clutch.

"I see you have made it to me, but why are you both tattered. Did you quarrel with each other during the last leg of the voyage?" Hikarge looked from the boy, still being held by his mate and the ground at Hikothe.

Hikothe spoke to answer, "We were attacked. The Dama from the neighboring cloister, with whom I assumed as ally, sent assassins to put an end to my life. We won the battle, but it would seem he has declared a silent war. I hate it has come to this. I still do not understand why he would not have simply dined with me and discussed his grievances. Nevertheless, I would have tried to forgive him if it was simply me in my old age, but he also tried to destroy the life of my grandson and heir. That is unforgivable. After we finish giving him a history lesson, I will visit the sneaky Dama at the cloister, Filar. And depending on his answers, it shall not be pleasant."

The blue dragon sat in silence for a moment then spoke, "Dama Nibut sent assassins like a coward. After we conclude speaking this evening with young Hikune, I shall fly you over there to converse with the Dama." The dragon had walked to large space, scrapped smooth from years of scale usage and settled. He told his visitors to sit as he retrieved his ancestor memories to retell the next phase of the houman history to Hikune.

"Well Hikune," began the blue dragon, "this is

the same story I had to tell your grandfather. He then brought his father, your great grandfather, and I recounted the events to him as best I could. I have told your father before you, and it will be my honor to release this knowledge to you.

"I believe Hikothe should have ended with the traitor Duvotch being consumed by my grandfather's power of lava."

Hikothe cleared his throat in agreement while young Hikune simply nodded.

"After that, Sherygha ordered some of the dragons that decided to spectate the fight to bring the boy Rynatch over to him. When they did he decreed, "As you have attacked the Governor of this world, so shall you be punished. I have already taken one of your hearts, now I shall also take one of your wings. You will forever be, at best, half a dragon. However, I am not heartless. As you three are the offspring of my oldest friend, I shall have King Dwarfe send more workers to my home. On the opposite side of my cave, I shall allow a cave to be built for you until you decide to claim your own cave for a clutch. Jysmun and Fyndesch, you will be able to leave when you please, but your disgraced brother cannot. Treat him well while he lives with you. As you are orphans, I shall look after you while you continue to grow. Though for now, I shall leave you alone to allow you time to grieve. We will be leaving in three days." Sherygha took a few steps, walking slow to not further his pain, then looked back and spoke, "I have told you my plans. If you decide to leave, I shall not stop you, excluding Rynatch. If you decide to go before I issue your punishment, when I find you, I will procure both of your wings, leaving you wholly grounded like a large white lizard. That is all, young dragons." Sherygha then trotted to the gathering of his mate, children, and houmans.

He went into the enormous shelter built for his family and rested. Shaman and a student he began teaching while in Zhivy known as "Shaman of Zhivy", began to work their "magic" and started healing him. The three days went by with a flurry. He could hear the raucous of center Zhivy breaking down tents, putting away camps, and destroying the pavilions that housed their various goods, services and workshops. Many times, the food, unable to be properly stored was given away to leaving families of isolated villages. He could hear and smell the commotion, but wanted no part of it. The giant black dragon loved to see houmans move and work, being alive as the High God intended, but the last days of visiting Zhivy were filled with sorrow. Another two of the first fifty dragons were void of life, and by his family. His oldest friend was killed by his children, because she was glamourized into attacking him. And to open old wounds, the High God was not returning to offer comforting words to put him at peace. It was a dreadful three days.

Nevertheless, on the morning of the third day, he rose and ate the large pile of food that had been collecting for him. He silently thanked Shaman for being an ever faithful friend and follower. Inside the meal were fragments of gold, the perfect metal to finish healing Sherygha's scales before he took the journey home. He again thanked Shaman for his hospitality and they silently headed to the door. When he released the hiding mechanism, he saw his children, along with the adopted Lypara. They were being cleaned and groomed by Vora, Shaman of Zhivy, and some of the other Ormaques that had relocated to the lake village that helped form the cloister Zhivy. As he became known a silence befell the gathering. None knew what to say. After a few moments his mate spoke for the group, "Wonderful proctor, we have been waiting your arrival. All preparations are completed, and whenever you decide fitting, we shall follow you to our home."

Sherygha did not verbally answer, but did the houman tradition of nodding his head up and down in agreement. Then he walked to the lake to drink some water. While there he heard voices. It was the three children of Rynesch, so he made his ears acute and listened to the ongoing conversation.

"It does not matter brothers," spoke the eldest Jysmun, "the great dragon has offered his graces and I believe we should receive them. You surely cannot blame him for taking your heart and soon your wing. You attacked him. If anything, you should forever be in his mercy that he did not kill you. Our mother told us that father was driven mad with jealousy and not to encumber ourselves for his fight. You did the exact opposite and this is the price that you must pay." The beautiful female dragon Jysmun paused, drinking in more of the water then continued, "I shall be going with him, learning all I can from the black dragon, and then living my eternal life. I am sad, truly, but am in no position to turn my tail up and show my waste hole at an offer of help and friendship. I strongly hope you will follow me, brothers."

She began to walk off when another voice spoke up. "I will not. I simply cannot follow dear sister. He has killed our father, and his snooty seed has killed my mother. With that ice casing still intact we cannot even see her one last time. I, my sibling, will find my own path. Then I will return when I am ready to even the score. I am Fyndesch, son of Duvotch and Rynesch the sky Queen. I will prosper regardless of what situation I am in. I am not as strong as you two now, but believe me, I will grow. And when I return, I will be able to battle any dragon I meet as I avenge my parents. Rynatch, my elder brother, will you be joining me or our dear white sister?"

Sherygha was not in a position to see, but a sole set of wing beats were retreating, as Fyndesch flew in the opposite direction. So two would take his offer, but one still wanted revenge. Sherygha decided those odds were okay with him as he returned to the others. As he bade his hosts a farewell he decided to pay Zharda a visit as well.

He entered the cave and saw her cleaning up a mess her toddler has created. "We are leaving Queen Zharda. I hope that one day you will not have to stay hidden and I, as well as my family gets to see you again. If you need any help from my clan please do not be afraid to send for my help. Your husband, Shaman, can always find me, as he has drunk of my blood." The large dragon breathed his celestial power over her one last time, hoping to prolong her ability to walk since he did not know how long the new elixir would last. He opened a smaller wound and let a bowl fill with his blood. "Tell Shaman to use my personal blood in his next elixir for you." He then retreated from the enclosure.

When he looked at the exit he noticed two smaller dragons had appeared, as expected. He looked over his ever growing family and decided it was time to leave, while the sun was high and they could enjoy the day as they leisurely flew home, accounting for his scarlet daughter. He knew she could not simply fly there as easily as the other dragons.

Just as Sherygha launched himself into the air Jysmun decided to follow. She caught up with the now surrogate father and glided alongside him. "I am sorry about what happened to my mother. I do not know why she decided to attack you, after she had already warned us about interfering with our father's battle. Either way, I and my brother thank you for your generosity. We will do whatever it is you ask, and hope to learn from you as well." She beat her wings softly along a warm breeze for a few strokes, and then added, "I personally want to thank you for sparing my brother's life. I know you could have killed him with more ease than some prey, yet you decided against it out of respect for my mother."

Sherygha turned to the young dragon flying beside him. She was around the same age as his children, but was the only dragon of that age he met with the same wisdom. Rynesch had tried to teach her clutch well. "You are quite wise young dragoness. You not only observe, but comprehend. I believe you and your brother shall get along very well with my clutch." Sherygha looked at the dragons flying ahead of him, seeing her brother, white and sapphire. With the slight glow from the sun he looked like a young version of his mother. His face and demeanor grew grim from the memory of losing his oldest friend. Then he added, "However, I will still hold true to my punishment of your brother. It is not my nature to recede on my promises." Then the dragon pulled away, beating his wings harder until he reached his daughter.

"How are your wings my beauty?" asked Sherygha.

"I am fine father, really. I only push them to achieve another high current. I mainly just float using the air swelling from my siblings beats like you taught me. Give me another twenty minutes and we can rest." She saw her father with a worried look in his eyes and looked back to see Jysmun still where he had left her and knew the secret conversation. She furthered, "I'm sorry father. I know she was your friend. We did the only thing we could think of to save you."

"Nonsense child," answered Sherygha. "It was the right thing to do. I'm lucky to have sired such powerful children. I would have been strong enough to defeat her, but between my already going battle, and the reluctance I had to fight her, there was no way I would have survived wholly intact." He grew weary again. "A few more minutes and we shall stop. I smell fresh water and would like a drink."

They flew and stopped and flew again. They each took turns using the harness and carrying Vora as they flew. It took a day and a half, faster this time than when traveling to the celebration. When they reached the cave they immediately called for the Uckleet families that has settled and built lives on Mageek after completing the cave for Sherygha and his clutch. He decided that he would also ask king Dwarfe for four more workers, as there would be two caves excavated instead of one, even though smaller. They settled in, and Sherygha explained the lifestyles of the inhabitants of Mageek. He explained how the dragons lived with the houmans and how everybody worked together to make everybody prosperous. Everyone found personal spots and slept in his cave for the night, and in the morning he would visit the home of the Uckleet.

In the morning Sherygha decided he would take Sherybi, being the strongest of his clutch, to procure the Uckleet members given by Dwarfe and assist in carrying the little houmans back. He and his son, both black and gold, though, still different, drank as much of the magic water as they could, and ate two of the enchanted fish each. They would fly hard and fast in the bright sun before the storm came. He could smell it in the air, though it was behind them. Truth be told, after the ordeal with the lightning, Sherygha had never wanted to fly in a storm again. He was never fond of it to begin with, and vividly remembering the strikes of lightning that left him for dead made him dread it even more.

"Son, hurry up and finish. We must each bring a rock of silver and a rock of gold to King Dwarfe. Last time I was more forceful as he had been rude to me. This time I shall offer the most prized metals on earth to gain the employment I seek. I will need four more Uckleet to assist in building the two caves for Rynesch's two heirs."

Guzzling down the last of the fish and water for their meal, Sherybi shook his body and outstretched his wings. "I am ready father. I will grab two silver and gold rocks and we can depart."

They each clutched the metals in their claws and took to the sky. The sun was high and bright. In the semi-clear sky they flew. The planet was growing with small settlements. However, the rest was a virtual paradise. It was full of forests of lush green plants and trees ranging from visually pleasing to poisonous to edible. Sometimes any mixture of the three could be found also. In the jungle were a multitude of wonderful animals that had evolved from previous beings. Then the grasslands were vast with rocks and streams and open for the much desired sun bathing. The green flowing grass river was soft and until the cold months very inviting for an afternoon nap. The mountains offered a cool rest and ice peaks for isolation. This is the world he wanted to ensure his many clutches would grow in. They would live the rest of their lives in a grand planet, made by to High God to offer luxury and pleasantness. If only he did not see the darker side of the second smartest species, the houmans. It could truly be paradise, and he would try his best to keep it as such.

The pair flew and flew. They beat hard and often. When their wings would tire, they would simply do as Shedrya advised, and gain higher altitude to glide on the air currents. It would eventually slow them down and they would have to push again, but it was the only way to keep from going down and taking an unwanted rest. It seemed a blur and before either of them realized they were approaching the large doors, now built of wood as well as gem stones, of the original cave of the Uckleet race and home of their king, Dwarfe.

"Halt dragons. What business do you have here?" asked one of the little guards at the gate slits.

"I am Sherygha, and have come to request an audience with King Dwarfe. This is my son behind me. His name is Sherybi, and will be watching the meeting as well. Tell old Dwarfe, I come to him in peace and expect the alike."

The guard stood there, stunned at the boldness of the large dragon. He hesitated for a moment, and then ran inwards to the labyrinth of tunnels. The two dragons waited for over ten minutes. Then another thirty passed. Growing frustrated Sherybi hit the door with his tail. It was solidly built, but with enough knocks and force he could break through. He roared and hit the door again. Sherybi jumped back and gathered his strength. He was about to let out a blast of ice when Sherygha struck him across the face with his tail.

"Be calm my son. A hot temper is always the first downfall of a dragon. I have not raised you to be so hot blooded. We shall wait another hour. After that, then we shall decide the next course of action. Now straighten up immediately."

Sherybi apologized and sat behind his father in obedience. He was looking at the door when a small figure grazed across his eye. He turned to the bushes but saw nothing. He heard nothing. After a moment he decided it was a small meal to be eaten later and looked back at the entrance. Sherygha suddenly roared and leapt into the air. He twirled and landed in the same spot he had just been viewing.

"Father I have just looked there. I thought it was something as well, but I assumed it was only a rodent fleeing from us."

Sherygha growled and dug around, slashing trunks of trees and upturning the brush. Then he stopped. He did not move for an instant, and then responded to his son, "You did look and hear in this direction. However you did not use all your senses; did you? Houmans have a peculiar smell, especially when they are frightened. I noticed you staring at the bushes with no movement, so I smelled the air. He was hiding in open view with this green leafy outfit. He set out to deceive us. That is not something I shall tolerate."

Sherygha lifted the tiny houman. King Dwarfe was no larger than the smallest digit on the claw of the enormous dragon. Most houmans were only the size of one normal digit of his claws, and the Uckleet were the shortest of all six races. He looked like a child being held by the black giant.

"Please do not kill me," pleaded the Uckleet king. "I was afraid you would break into my palace again. I was hoping to lure you away and ensure the safety of my people."

Sherygha laughed loudly. "I see you have brought two sacks with you. Both filled with precious gold and stones of value. You were not thinking of your people, but yourself. You did not lure me away but attempted to escape. And if my son had not sensed you, I am sure you would have left without a word."

He took the little man to the same slit he talked through. When a guard appeared he ordered him to open the gates. Fearful, the little people did as they were asked. He walked through the gate and summoned the elders of the founding families immediately. When they all arrived he began, "I am the same dragon that caused damage a decade ago. I have again come to seek the aid of your king, and again, he has tried to trifle with me. So I will first rid you of the incompetent king, and then I shall do business with the council." The large black dragon motioned to his son. Sherybi brought the large rocks of silver forward and placed them in front of the watching council. "I brought payment for what I ask, just like any other, but was treated with disrespect, yet again. I warned him last time that if I returned and he deceived or misled me, I would kill him. I, AGAIN, came for business, and found a fleeing king. He was leaving you all to my wrath. I do not find this fair, so here are his sacs of wealth he had with him." Sherygha tossed the large bags to the ground and the jewels and gold and silver spilled out of them onto the floor. He then stood as tall as he could and spoke with a deeper voice, "As punishment, he shall come with me. After he has worked his debt, I will decide whether to kill him or not. Now, I also need another four workers to build again, as I need another cave created from the mountainside of my home."

The elders quickly spoke amongst themselves. They

summoned the four members that would depart with the dragons. Then in a twist, the council brought forward king Dwarfe's eldest son. They took the crown that was lodged in the bag and placed it on his head. Dwarfe, now dethroned, yelled in anger. He grabbed a knife of stone out of his pocket and lunged at his son. He stabbed him in the chest repeatedly. Sherygha grabbed the past king and tossed him into his mouth, eating him in one singe gulp. He then blew over the young king. Alas, it was too late; the boy was dead, by his own father's hand no less. The council ordered his body taken away. They then took the crown to his second son, who had now arrived to see the commotion.

"All hail King Xiver, second son to former king Dwarfe. Ruler of the Uckleet"

The crowd chimed in, completely in unison. "All hail King Xiver. All hail King Xiver."

Sherygha looked around. They all applauded the new king, who still stood there in astonishment. As a second son he was trained in the royal way, but never thought he would become king. The most he had hoped for was a settlement of burrowed mountains to govern; now he had taken the crown, created by the High God himself for his grandfather's, grandfather's grandfather. The very first king of the Uckleet; also created by the High God himself. The dragon showed his respect and lowered his head to the new king. Sherybi followed. Sherygha spoke while lifting his head, "Dear noble king, I wish you many years like your father. I hope this will be the beginning of a new era for your people in this world. As always, I am here to assist you when needed." He looked around, seeing some with joy, by many, including members of the high council, looking on with disdain and contempt. He then added, "To help your people, I offer this also, so we may start fresh business between the Uckleet and my dragons." Sherygha motioned again and Sherybi brought forward a large rock of gold and offered it to the young King.

The council offered their thanks and retreated deeper into the cave, leaving the new King and his guard at the cave opening. Xiver was still stunned but was trying to show his appreciation to his subjects. Sherygha heard multiple Uckleet houmans talking as they retreated. Many were saying they were true to the name of Dwarfe and would calling themselves Dwarves from there on to signify their loyalty. He found it odd, but as usual, decided not to interfere with the inner workings of the houmans. It would unfold as it always did.

He bade the new king farewell and reminded him that not everyone is happy when new kings are appointed. Sherygha told him to always be kind, however always weary. Or his days will be short lived. He and his son left to hunt while the four members packed their belongings and said their goodbyes. The two dragons returned to the cave, teeth and lips crimson from the warm blood of fresh kills. They grabbed the four small houmans needed for the excavation. They learned that just like last time, they were criminals that would earn their freedom upon completion of the project. The group flew to the horizon. They did not stop until they reached home, still taking alternate paths to confuse the hired houmans. It had been a long day, and the dragon decided he would deal with the new Uckleet residents in the morning. He told his mate of all that transpired, drank from a tub of Mageek water, and slept.

****

The years turned into decades. The decades turned into a century. Then it repeated again and again. Sherygha stood atop a high mountain one night while his life mate lay asleep inside a cave they created near the jagged peak. From the vantage he examined the world below; reflecting on how much the world had changed over the past three centuries. The races had mixed so much that they all seemed to share the same traits as the other races, however only a select few had achieved true houman status due to the houman nature to mate with their own race. Every so often, while touring Choi he would see a faint and unusual aura surrounding a houman. These people were dangerous. Once they completed what the High God intended they would be able to yield immense power. Luckily most of his Ormaques stayed to themselves. However, some had mated with other races. Their children would do the same. Some stayed with whatever race they stopped at, but others still mated with other races. The term clan had become more prevalent. The clan was a family, or group of families that shared a characteristic. These clans were becoming the norm as the houmans spread rapidly across the land. They were not only growing in population, but also wisdom.

Fyndesch had seen the individuals with the same

aura. They looked and smelled different than regular houmans. He tried to heal a powered arfaet man that had attacked him. The silver and ruby dragon decided that if he healed the houman, he could make him his slave and tender like the ones that lived with Sherygha. He breathed his celestial power on the houman, however, it instead gave the man immense power. Not enough to kill the large dragon, but stronger than any other houman. He repeated the process with another powered Arfaet. He then searched and gathered a dark Mylare and Uckleet of colored aura. He gifted them with power as well.

Fyndesch had amassed a small force of powered houmans, able to do his bidding. He attacked many villages, looting everything of value. Knowing that her brother was becoming as evil as their father, Jysmun decided to stop him. However she could not attack him with his four houman protectors. She left, wounded and defeated. She was laying down when a houman walked by. He smelled like the stink species, yet, with a dragon's influence. She looked up and could see the aura surrounding him. It was a Norfex man. Suddenly another walked up, tall and pale. A Mylare man with an aura as well. They were cousins, both living in the same village. She offered them power if they would use it for the betterment of the houman race. They agreed, taking the power in and learning how to wield it from their dragon master.

However, the two siblings decided not to declare war on each other. Fyndesch had four generals, but by getting their power from him, were also weak, like him. Jysmun, set to stop him, had only empowered two generals, but by having her power were naturally stronger than their adversaries. Thus neither wanted to fight the other, and both had a disadvantage to declaring a full scale war.

Sherygha looked to the dark sky. Stars twinkled in the massive space as he pondered about his creator. He missed his guidance. Sherygha looked to the left and saw a large and beautiful full moon. It had the slightest touch of red and seemed so close he could fly there in minutes. It was shrouded behind dark clouds floating by, leaving only a ration of it visible to the onlooker. A storm was coming on the horizon; the wise dragon was sure, smelling the rain in the air. However, he was not yet sure how true the words were. He sat there under the stars on the icy mountain peak staring at the portion of the bright moon. He did not know the consequences of the sibling dragons' actions. He did not know how the world would fare. He did not even know his next actions to protect the world from the new threats. He did know one thing however; a storm was brewing on the horizon.

ORIGINAL HOUMAN RACES

HUFORE— Physically close to weak and feeble. High reproduction and population growth. Highly Nomadic. Largest area of expansion from roaming. Assisted the other races in advancement and some technology. / Black eyes, brown skin, burnt orange hair.

ORMAQUES - 2nd in intelligence only to Hufore. Can generally be found in bodies of water or caves and forests. Shape shifters. Produce and use potions and poisons. Least intermingled race. / (natural form) Purple eyes, grey skin, Black hair.

UCKLEET – Short, stout and strong. Generally works in mines, caves and trade. Hairy, long beards, (often beaded). Strong hierarchy. / Hazel eyes, rosy skin, light brown hair. (Though often black from living in caves)

MYLARE - Very tall, pale, lean. Acute hearing. Swift runners. Rarely unhealthy thus highly increased life span. Divided race: dark and light versions. Dark Mylare have sharpened nails and filed teeth for fangs/ Pale Mylare: Red eyes, pale skin, white and green hair; Dark Mylare: Green eyes, tinted pale skin, white and varying color hair.

ARFAET - Broad bodied. Lowest intellect. Blood thirsty. Always at war, sometimes amongst other villages of Arfaet people. Unkempt and wanton. Warriors and conquerors. Crave power. First to betray dragons. Also known as Dragon-Slayers. Greyish blue eyes, olive skin, blonde hair.

NORFEX – Tall, but not as much as Mylare, broad bodied, but less than the Arfaet. 2nd largest roaming area. Most intermingled race. Least pure bred race (often turned into slaves.)/ Brown eyes, red hair, Golden/Caramel skin.

MAIN DRAGONS AND CHARACTERS

SHERYGHA- Enforcer. 2 opposite elements for balance. Almost as old as Rynesch. Black with Gold tint and edges. {Fire and Ice}

RYNESCH- Oldest Dragon on Earth. Leader of Dragonkind. Sometimes called the Sky Queen / Silver with Sapphire tint and edges. {Wind}

HIKARGE- Oldest and strongest present day dragon. Is paired with Hikothe from birth as his carrier. Reviver of Dragonkind on Earth. / Blue with dark Gold tint and edges. {Lightening}

HIKOTHE- The Ruler of Aimone. Strongest and oldest Dragon rider. Grandfather to Hikune. Rider of the grand dragon, Hikarge (also his son's name)

HIKUNE- Grandson of Hikothe. A dragon tender. Future rider of dragon in the egg. Next ruler of the cloister, Aimone.

ZHARDA- First queen of the Hufore race.

SHAMAN- Strongest of the Ormaques.

GLOSSARY

VILLAGE- An area of a race or groups of races, generally created by 10 or more families. Each village has an Elder that governs it.

CLOISTER- Group of villages banded together under one monarch. Cloister varies on amount of villages added. Each cloister is ruled by a sole monarch.

AIMONE- The Cloister is ruled by Dragon rider, Hikothe. It contains over fifty villages of varying sizes.

ZHIVY- The first cloister of Choi. Beginning of the Houman race.

CHOI- The name of the massive, single continent that occupied earth before the great dragon war caused it to separate.

DAMA- King or ruler of a village cloister.

CLAUPINE- Largest River of the continent. Supports multiple Houmans. Used as a means of direction.

Excerpt from book two,

THE HOUMAN RACE: WAR

When the duo reached the encampment of Mylare they were met with screams. Blood and death was in the air. The sounds of weapons destroying flesh could be heard in multiple directions. Sherygha dashed towards the commotion. He stopped when he saw a group of Arfaet men cornering a young dragon. He was silver and ruby, and eating rocks and mouthfuls of soil that was around him. He whipped his tail at the approaching men with no effect. There were already marks on him from the dragon forged weapons and now that all of the Mylare were either injured or dead, the entire group focused on the dragon.

"I will kill you all!" boomed the enraged Sherygha to the group. They all changed focus from the little silver dragon to the enormous black and gold. Fear struck them as they realized who he was. Sherygha leapt in to the air, beating his wings swiftly and powerfully. In the air he roared, vehemently and full of malice. "Gather your brother; I will deal with this group of repulsive Houmans." Jysmun nodded and ran through the trees to get to her brother. She released a blast of water at the group, pushing them away from the crouching injured Fyndesch. Sherygha was flying low enough now to inflict direct damage. Seeing the water, he blew hard, icy air at the group. Many were frozen; others became too stiff to move, but had not died yet. The dragon landed and began breaking the frozen warriors with his claws and tail. He was in a berserk trance, clawing, biting and crushing anyone he saw move, including a few Mylare. The old dragon had spent the past day remembering his old friend, and here the Arfaet were, attacking her youngest child.

"This is Fyndesch, youngest of the sky queen's children. How dare you attack him? I will kill you all for your insolence!" Sherygha breathed in a large amount of air and spewed fire at the remaining four Arfaet who were trying to escape. The oldest one jumped to the ground and used a dying mylare man for cover. When he stood to face the enraged dragon, Sherygha saw a burn mark covering half of his face.

"I have met you before, houman. Dragons have great memories, and mine is of the best. We did battle before and I gave you that scar as a warning. I told you to never hunt dragons again. I spared your life so you could warn your brethren. However, you mistook my kindness for weakness. I will not make that mistake twice."

The arfaet man began to tremble at the memory of his face burning. For a time he did stop hunting dragons, but old habits are hard to break, and selling dragon parts was lucrative. Now, standing in front of the giant dragon again, he wished he tried harder to remain a humble farmer. Sherygha jerked his tail and knocked the man back down. He leapt on top of him and dug a claw into the man's stomach. He made sure not to rip open his heart, ensuring he feel the excruciating pain.

A livid Fyndesch ran up to the dragon and hit his hind leg with his tail horns. "I will devour him. I do not need your or my sister's help." Fyndesch stood above the screaming Arfaet and brought down both claws on his broad shoulders. He wrapped his still slender tail around the man's head, pulling out the bulk of his long, wanton blonde hair. "Thank you for being my meal," he hissed in the man's ear. Then he bit off a large piece of the man's dirty leg, swallowing it whole. He waited a moment, relishing in the calamitous screams of the dismembered houman. The silver dragon dug his claws even further in, ensuring the houman could not move and began eating his insides, while he was still alive. When he finished he looked down at the man with the half burnt face. His eyes were still open, his breathing was extremely faint. The Arfaet warrior had went into a state of shock.

"Kill him and move on," pleaded the watching Sherygha, feeling sorrow for the little dragon. "His punishments were just, now end his misery and let him die." Fyndesch looked at the dragon and began to hiss. He growled, low and menacing, then placed the houman down gently, preserving what life he could take from him later…

BIOGRAPHY

Warren Cohen, Jr. is an up and coming author in a new generation of authors. He graduated from Claflin University with a degree in Music Performance. When he was younger, he had a passion for reading in all genres. The varied styles of writing are what influenced him when writing The Houman Race: Birth. As an up and coming author, he hopes to soon be able to solely write for his readers. He lives in Columbia, SC and is married with a son, Warren, III.

Feel free to visit my website
sscohenjr.wix.com/authorwarrencohen

Made in the USA
Columbia, SC
02 April 2025

56034076R00148